RAMION

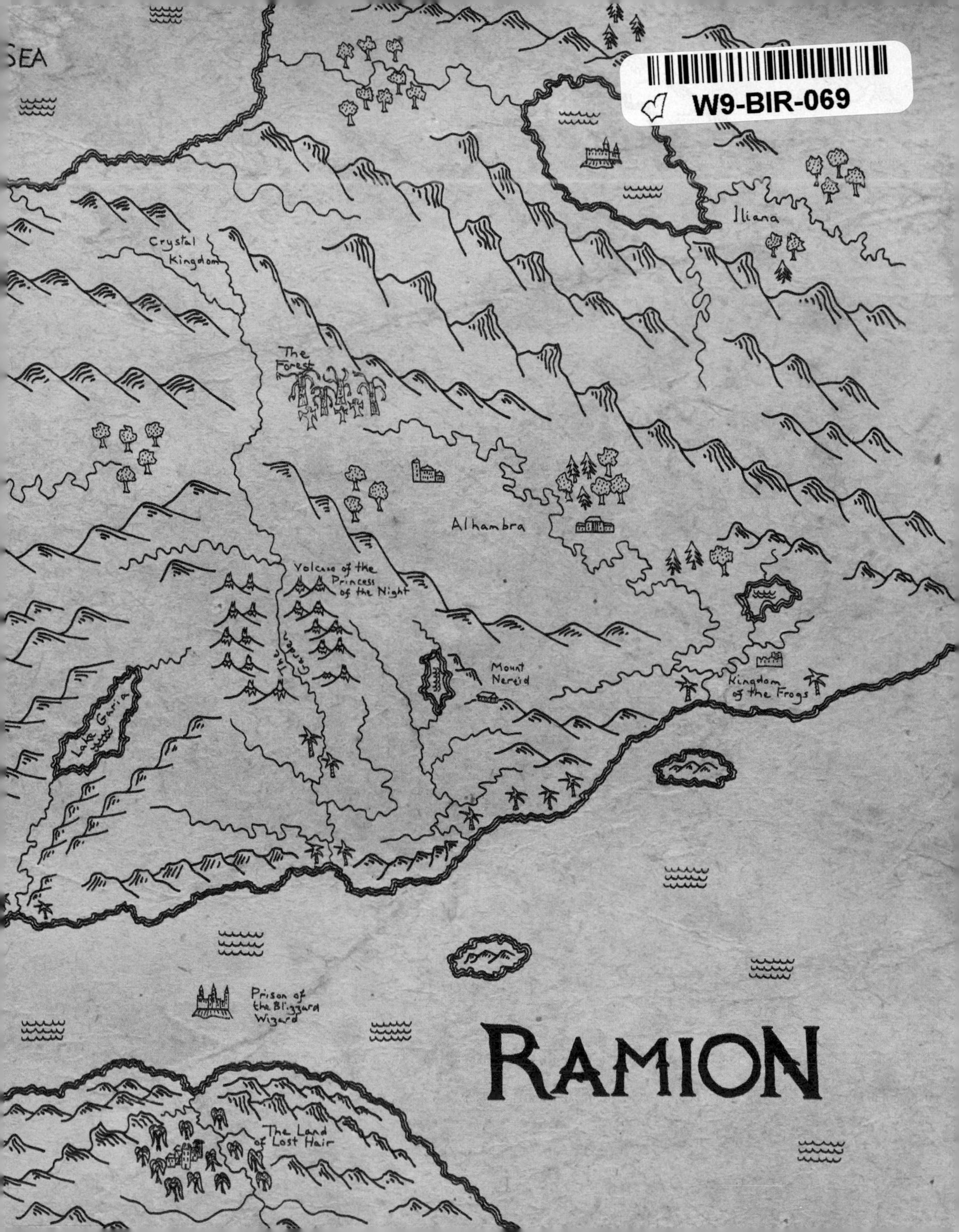
SEA
Crystal Kingdom
Iliana
The Forest
Alhambra
Volcano of the Princess of the Night
Lake Garia
Mount Nereid
Kingdom of the Frogs
Prison of the Blizzard Wizard
The Land of Lost Hair
RAMION

CREATURES OF THE FOREST

Published by
Perronet Press
www.ramion-books.com
Copyright © Text and illustrations
Frank Hinks 2018

A CIP record for this book is available from the British Library

ISBN: 9781909938144

Printed in China by CP Printing Ltd.
Layout by Jennifer Stephens

TALES OF RAMION

CREATURES OF THE FOREST

FRANK HINKS

Perronet

2018

TALES OF RAMION

THE GARDENER

Lord of Ramion, guardian and protector

SNUGGLE

Dream Lord sent to protect the boys from the witch Griselda

JULIUS
ALEXANDER
BENJAMIN

Three brothers who long for adventure

SCROOEY-LOOEY

Greedy, rude, half-mad rabbit, a friend of the boys

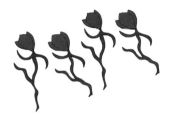

PRECIOUS PLANTS

*Have the power to reverse
evil magic*

RACING RACOONS

*Should have been rancid racoons,
but the spell went wrong*

DUCKY ROCKY

*Lives at the bottom of a pond,
source of knowledge*

GRISELDA THE GRUNCH

A witch who longs to eat the boys

THE DIM DAFT DWARVES

Julioso, Aliano, Benjio, Griselda's guards

BORIS

Griselda's pet skull, strangely fond of her

SCARY SCOTS

Five minutes of their sound and a boy will explode

THE GNARLED OLD MAN

Keeper of the Forest, not nice at all

VENOMOUS VAMPIRES

Very snooty, only want to drink your blood

HEAD GOBLIN

Keeper of the Lost Magic Office

CHAPTER ONE

The boys ran with Scrooey-Looey down to the river, over the bridge on to the water-meadow and jumped into a boat.

Julius took one oar, Alexander the other and began to row up river. Benjamin and the rabbit sat in the prow and quickly fell asleep. They rowed upstream until they reached a cave.

"It looks very dark," said Julius.

"I don't like it," cried Alexander.

"Let's go back," added Benjamin, who had awoken with a start.

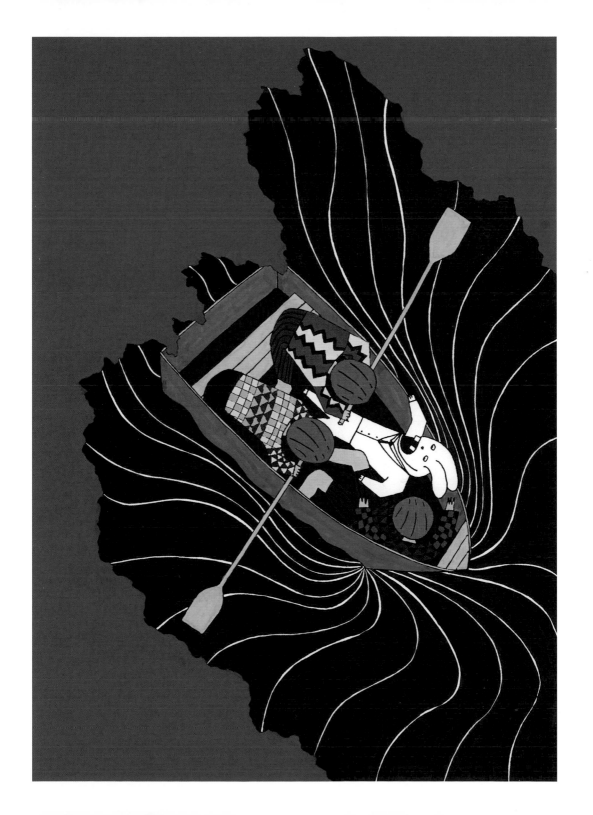

Julius and Alexander tried to turn the boat, to row back to the water-meadow, but it would not turn: it headed upstream by itself.

The boys and the rabbit huddled together in the bottom of the boat as it travelled upstream through the cave, the light of the entrance becoming smaller and smaller as the boat travelled faster and faster.

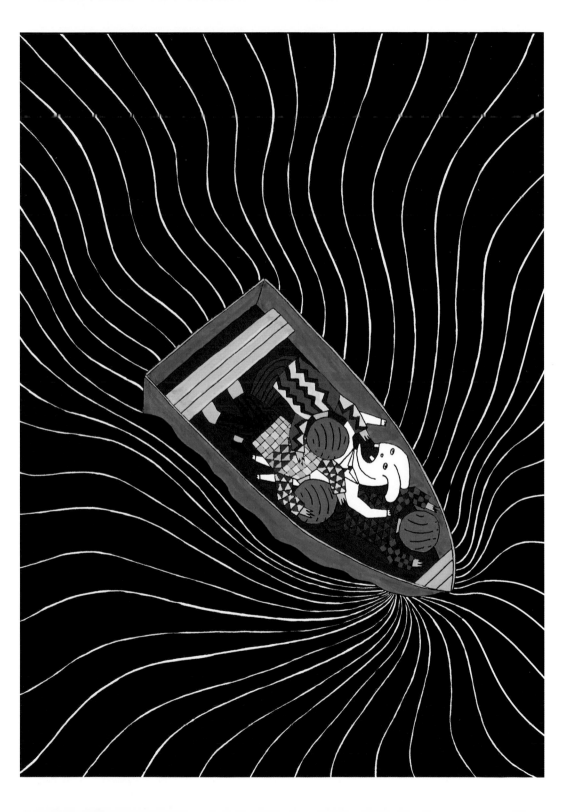

The boat stopped at a landing jetty in a vast cavern, stone steps rising up towards a faint green light. They got out of the boat and full of fear walked towards the steps.

A figure emerged from the sickly light.

"Welcome! Welcome!" cried the witch Griselda. "I am very pleased to see you."

Drawn by the power of Griselda's magic, the boys and Scrooey-Looey climbed the steps, left the dark cavern and entered the family vault, deep below the ruined tower.

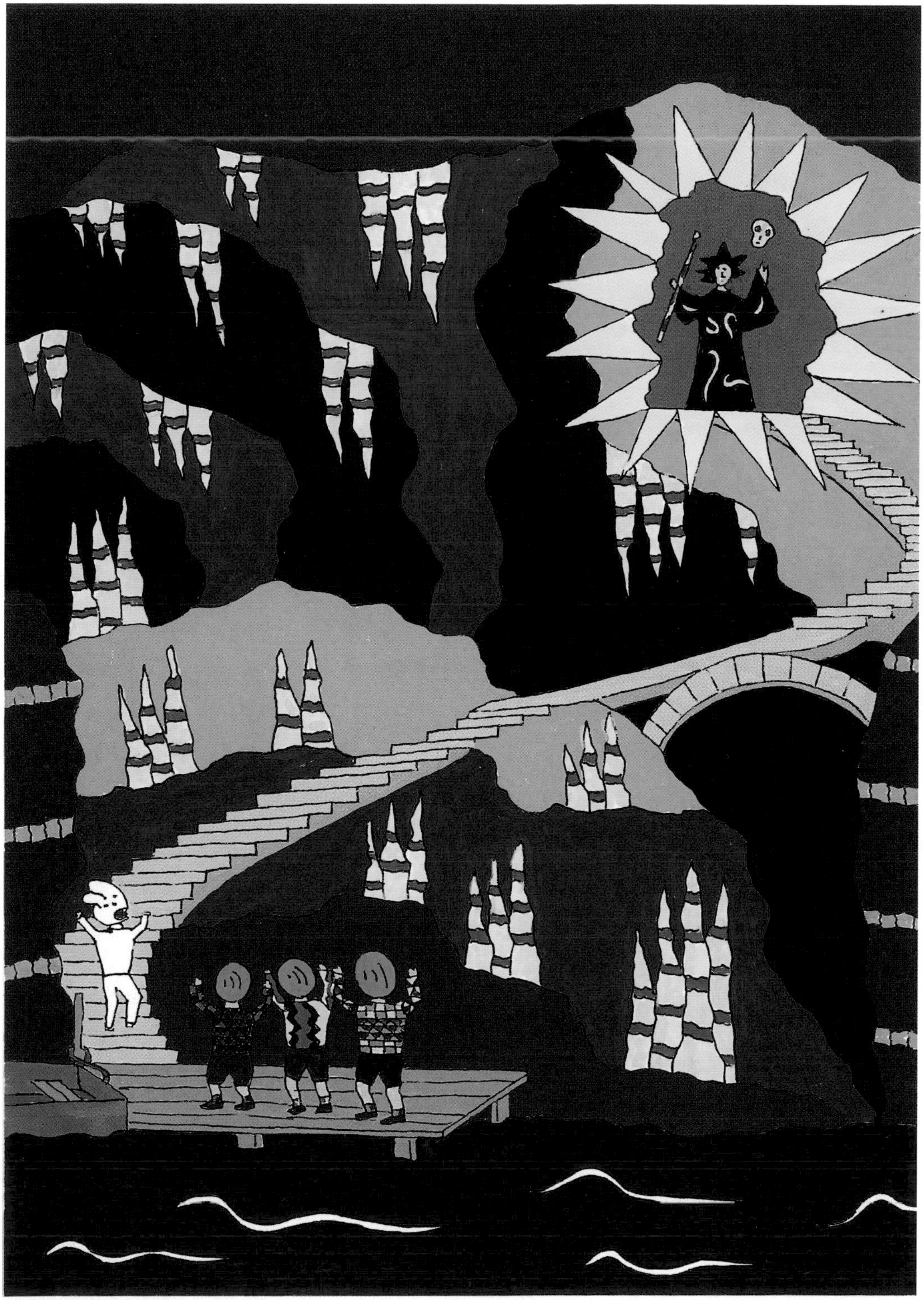

Griselda's dead ancestors stood in glass tanks, their flesh preserved in special fluid. Their evil spirit bubbled up through tubes stuck in their heads and was collected in dark bottles, a lovely drink (or so Griselda thought).

"Let me introduce you to Baron Rufus de Grunch, the founder of the family," said Griselda pointing to a bearded man standing in a glass tank, axe and spear in hand. "He was very fond of boys."

"She means he ate them," whispered Scrooey-Looey, as the boys and rabbit hurried out of the family vault, through the dungeon, out of the hall, into the glade deep within the forest.

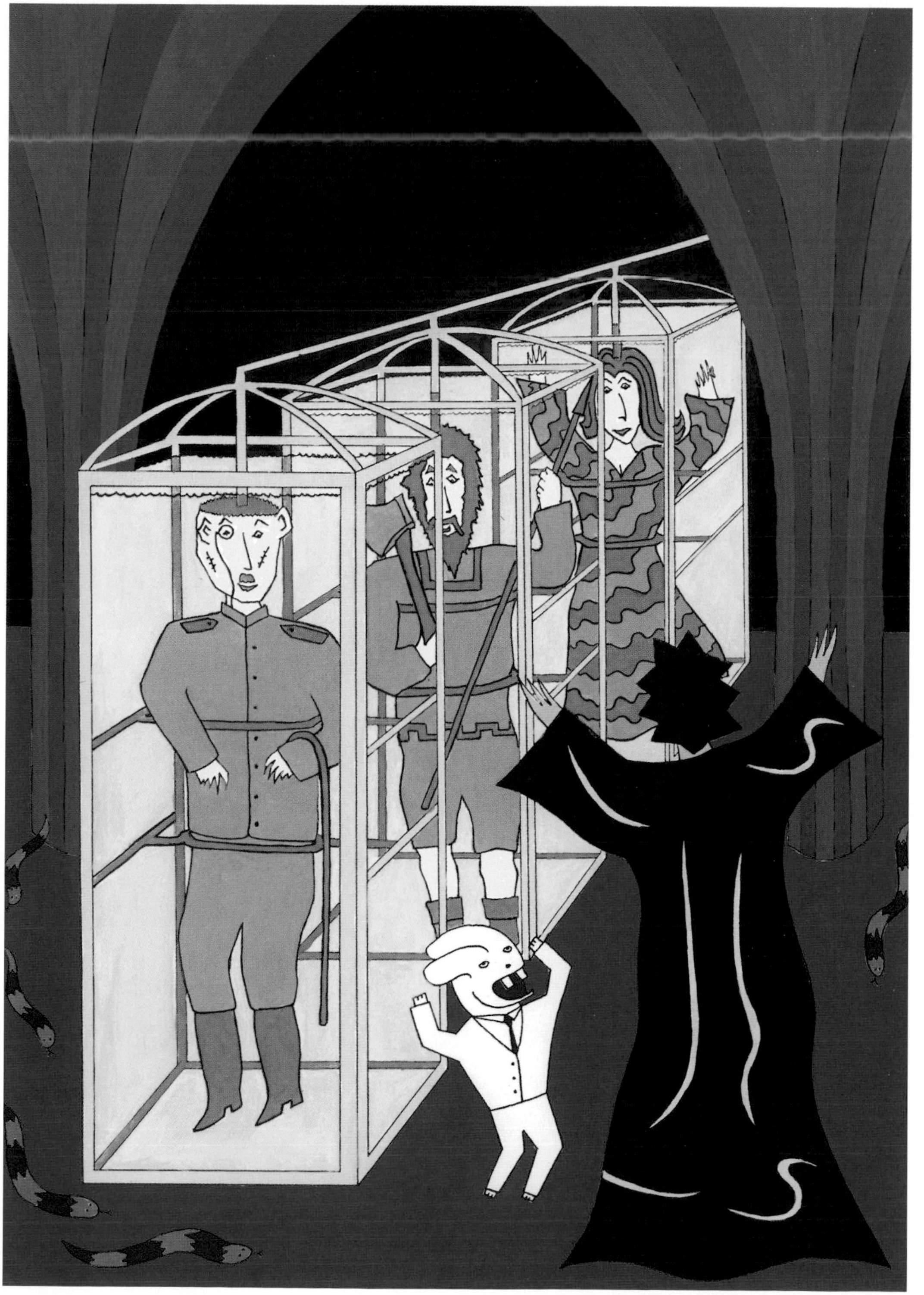

"Guards, come here!" bellowed Griselda. The three dwarves came running. "Put them in the cages, fatten them up, cook them for supper." Griselda went back into the tower leaving the Dim Daft Dwarves to get to work.

The boys fought hard. By the time the dwarves, Julioso, Aliano and Benjio, got the boys in the cages and fed them with the fattening mixture they were tired out. Griselda had left her magic staff beside the magic cauldron.

"Roasting, stewing and toasting boys is hard work. Let's cook them by magic," suggested Julioso, who was dim and did not know you cannot cook boys by magic: there is too much fun and wildness in them.

The Dim Daft Dwarves were puzzled: in none of Griselda's books could they find a spell for cooking boys. In the end they said the spell for cooking unicorns (changing the word 'unicorn' to 'boys and rabbit'). What happened next was surprising. All the snakes and creepy spiders in the glade got up and started ballroom dancing and the boys and Scrooey-Looey disappeared.

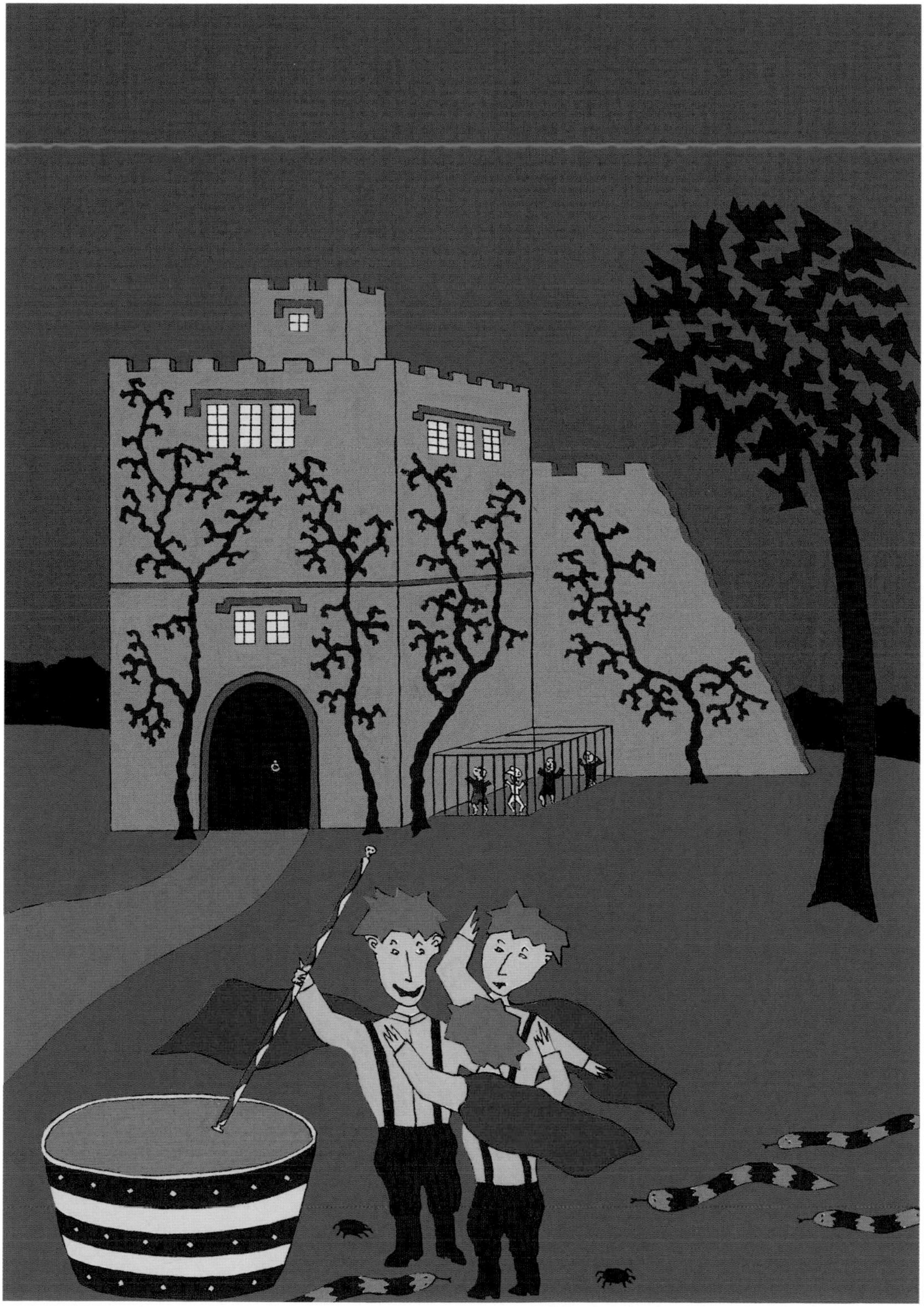

Chapter Two

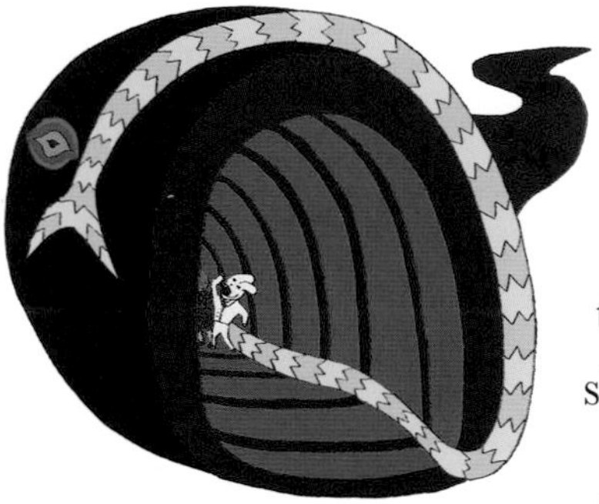

The boys and the rabbit were in what looked like a lost luggage office, except that instead of umbrellas there were top hats, silk handkerchiefs and magic wands.

Goblins hurried in, saw Scrooey-Looey and groaned: "Not another rabbit. Magicians are always losing rabbits."

The goblins seized Scrooey-Looey by the arms and threw him out the door. This made the boys very angry.

"You can't do that."

"That's Scrooey-Looey."

"He's our friend."

The goblins ignored them. "Now what have we here?" They looked carefully at the brothers and consulted a book. "Boys. It says here that magicians are forbidden to make boys disappear. If these three boys are part of an illegal act perhaps the magician will not dare to claim them. In three months we can sell them in the market. Lock them up."

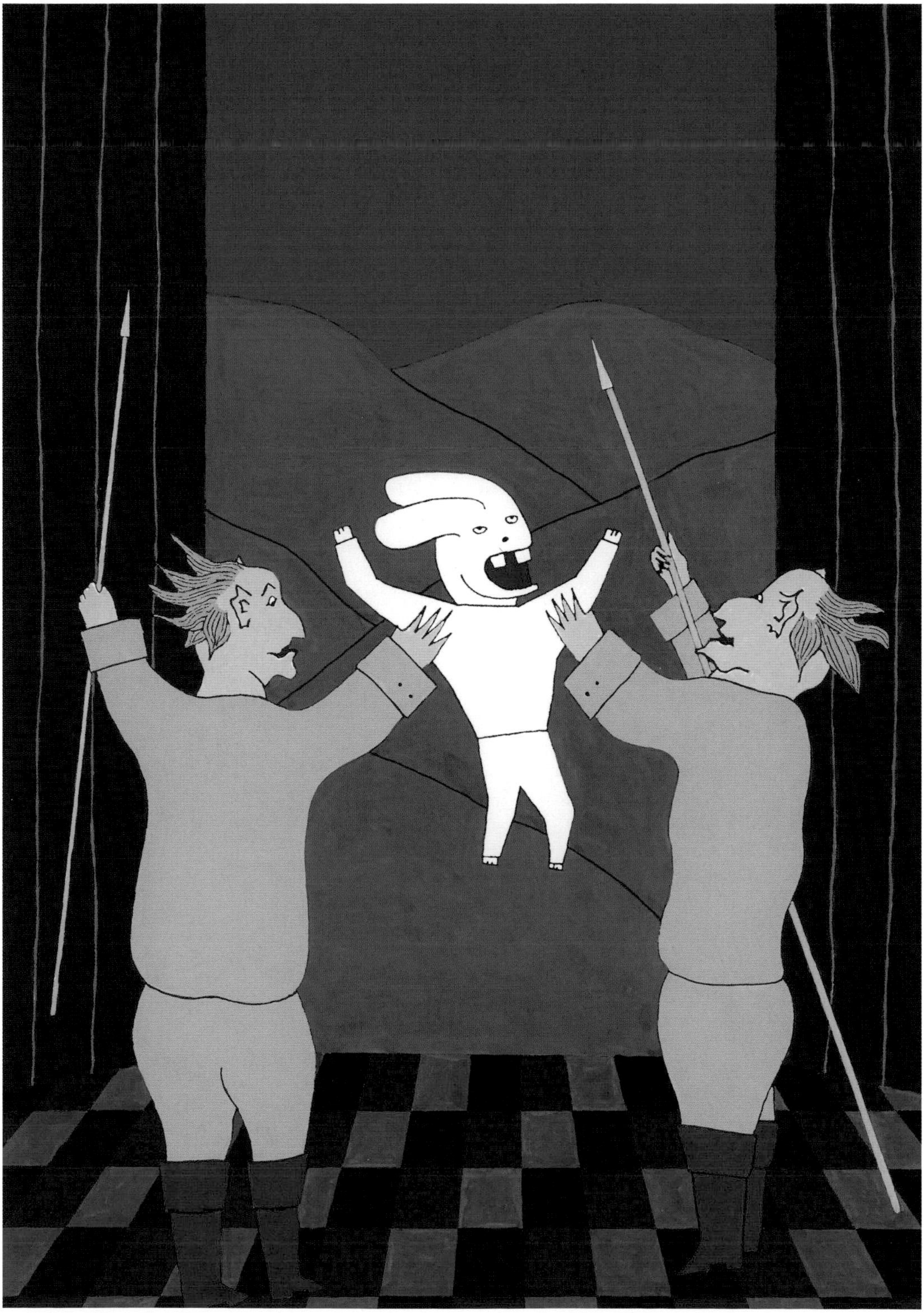

The goblins seized the boys and locked them in the strongroom, where they found a lady sawn in two, waiting patiently, her top half knitting, her bottom half practising a tap dance.

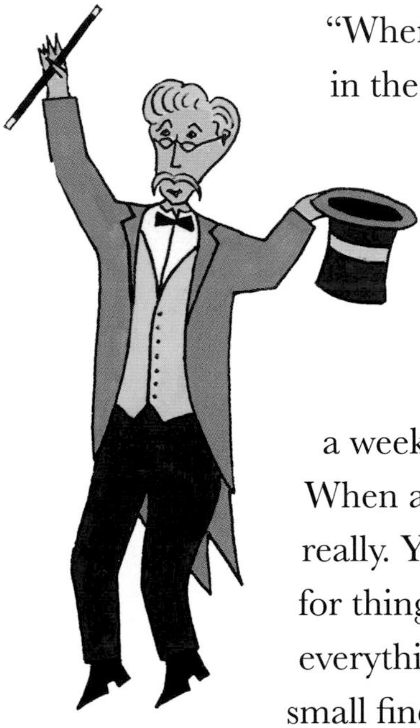

"Where is Jerry?" she sighed. "I left the supper in the oven. If he doesn't hurry, it will be burnt." She continued knitting and dancing, talking all the time:

"Who is Jerry? My husband. A magician. The most useless magician in the world. I end up here once or twice a week. Where are we? The Lost Magic Office. When a spell goes wrong you end up here. Sensible, really. You can't go hunting through the universe for things which have been magicked by mistake. So everything travels here. The magician comes, pays a small fine, and collects his lost property or assistant."

"What happens if he does not come?"

"Oh, after three months if you have not been collected, they sell you in the market."

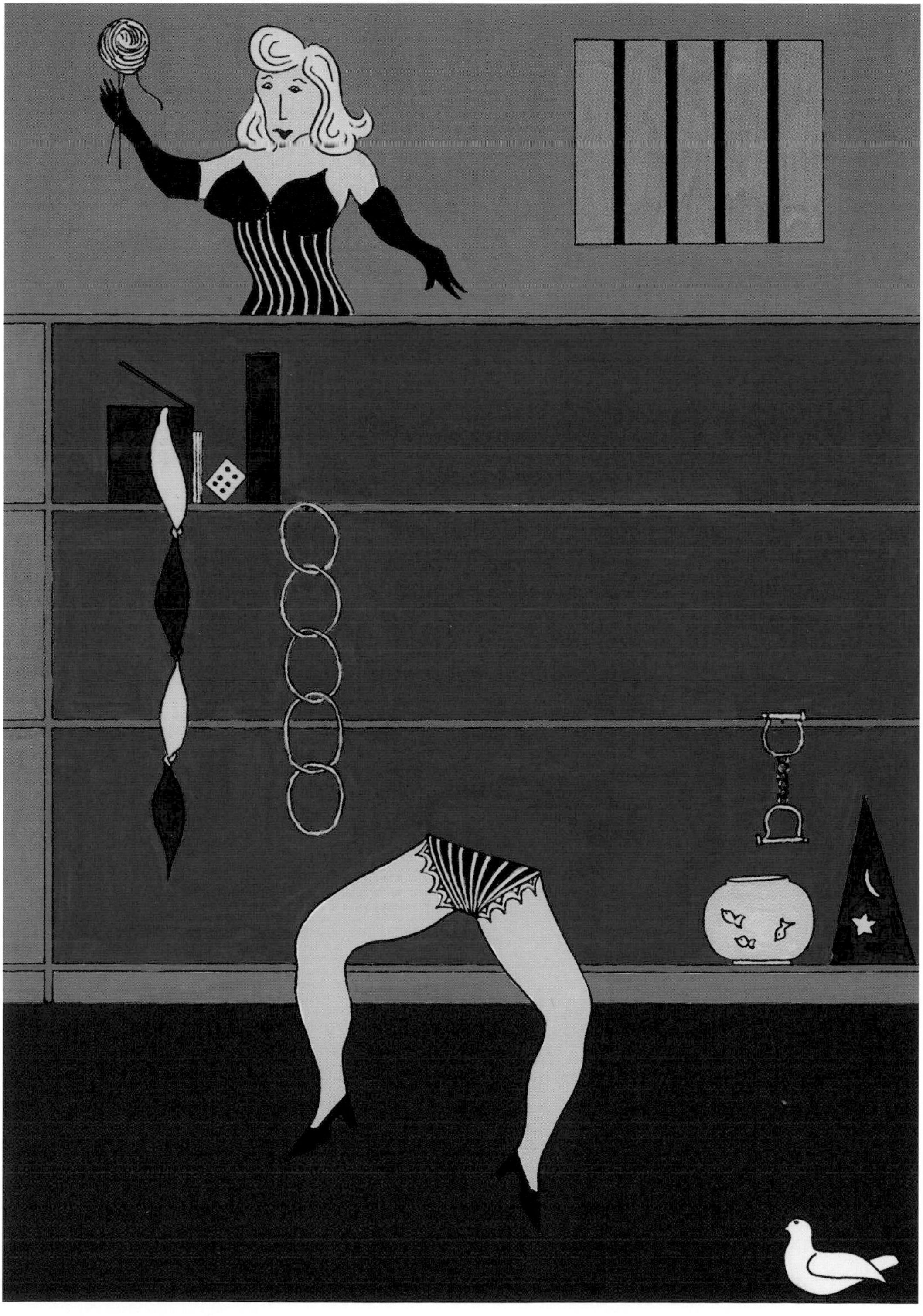

She continued talking. "Only the magician who magicked you here can get you out. What was her name? Griselda! Not a nice name. Not nice at all. Would not go down well with our audience. Jerry is the Great Fernando. I'm his assistant Esdermelda. Sounds better than Jerry and Sylvie. Perhaps this Griselda will come and get you out."

"We do hope not," said the boys. "We would prefer to be sold in the market."

The door opened and a little man in a top hat scurried in.

"My dear, I am so sorry. Such a silly mistake."

"Never mind. Just put me together before the supper's burnt."

The little man raised a magic wand and the two parts of Sylvie joined together.

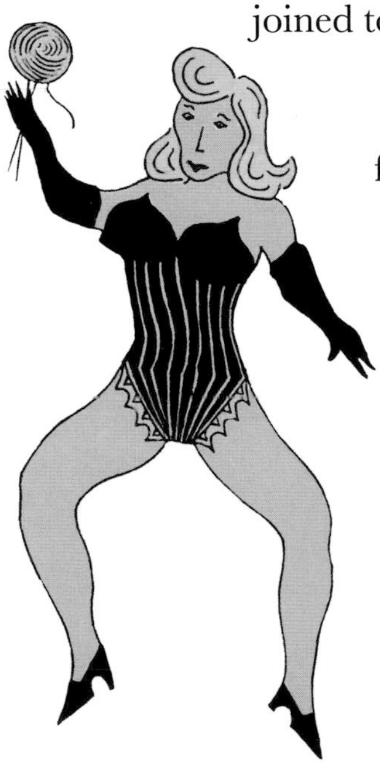

"Thank goodness for that," said Sylvie. "I never feel quite right when I am sawn in two."

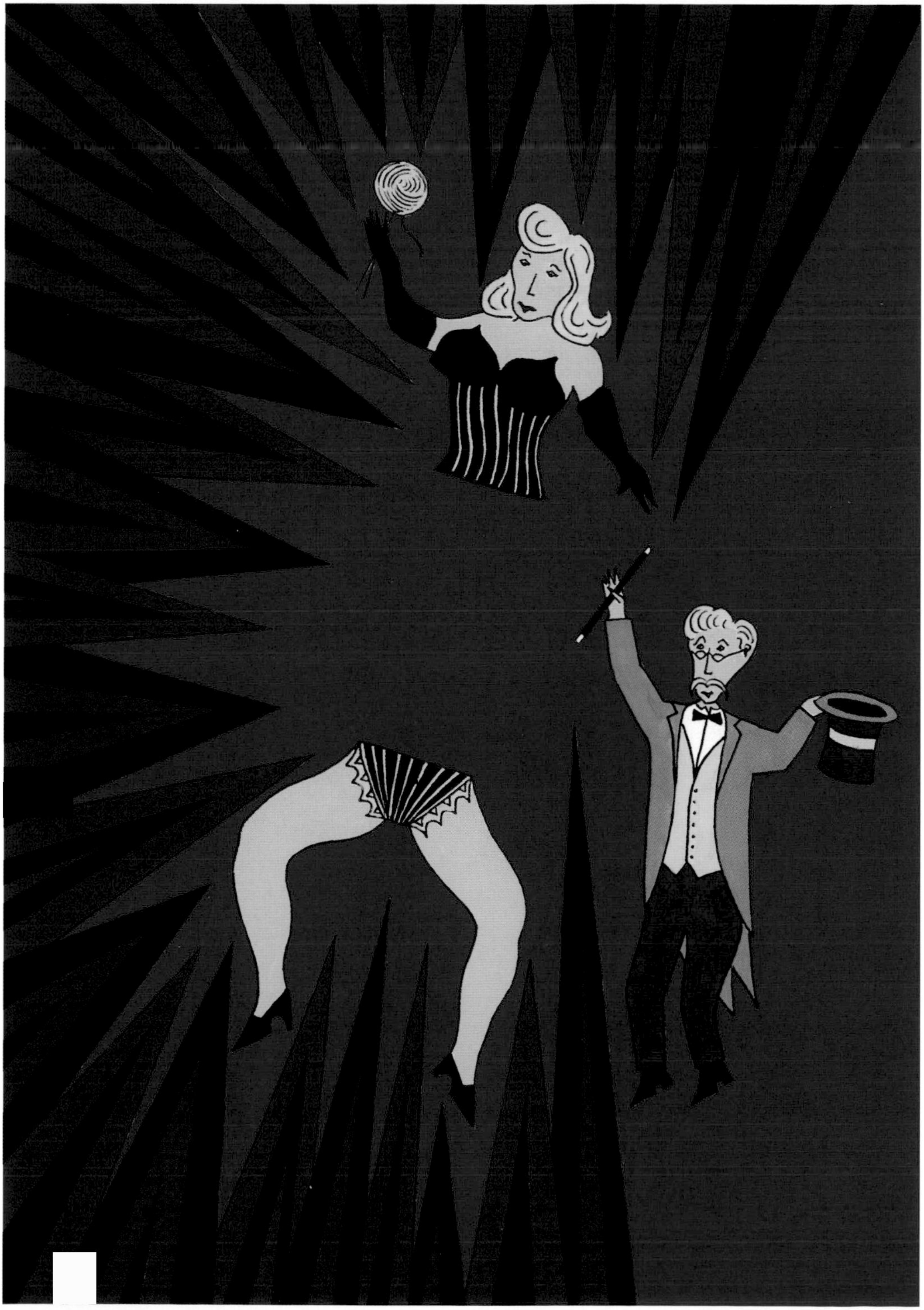

The boys were miserable.

"Either we are collected by Griselda or sold in the market."

"A very gloomy outlook."

"Not good at all."

"Where is Scrooey-Looey?" asked Benjamin. "Perhaps he can get us out."

The boys looked out of the window (which had heavy bars). "There he is. Scrooey-Looey!" the boys all shouted.

Scrooey-Looey turned, waved, squeaked excitedly, "They've just opened a new lettuce bar," and ran off.

Time passed slowly. Once or twice a week Sylvie appeared, sometimes whole, sometimes in two parts. She cheered them up.

"Hello boys. Still here. Where is that rabbit friend of yours? Still at the lettuce bar? What a shame."

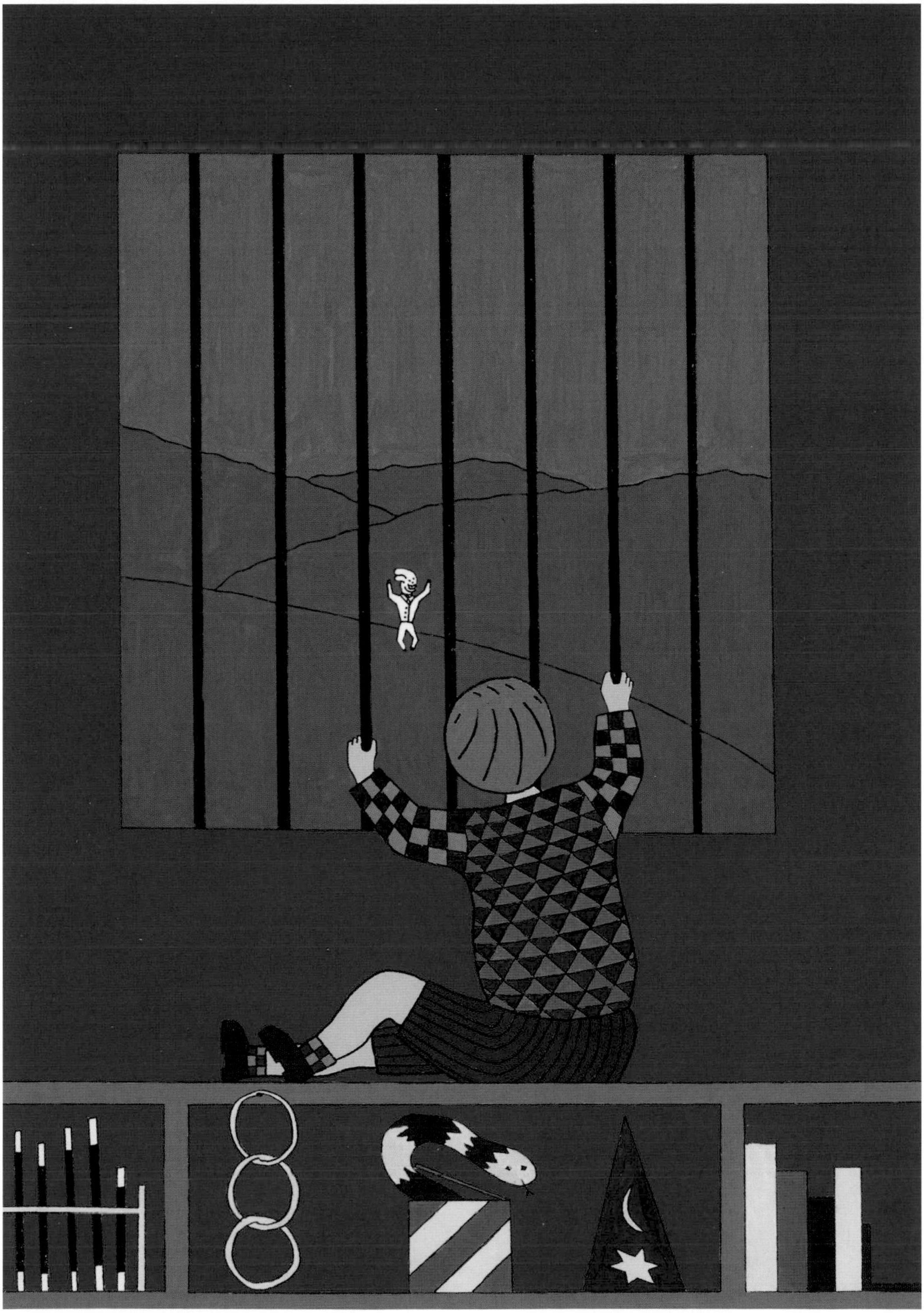

One day the boys heard the sound of shouting from the office outside the strongroom: Griselda was trying to claim them.

"Madam," said a goblin politely, "that would be against the rules. They were magicked here by three dwarves. Only the dwarves can claim them. Madam, you are not a dwarf."

"Of course I am not a dwarf," shrieked Griselda. "The dwarves belong to me. They are my property."

"That does not change Rule 33(2)(b)," said the goblin. "Only the person who magicked the property can reclaim it."

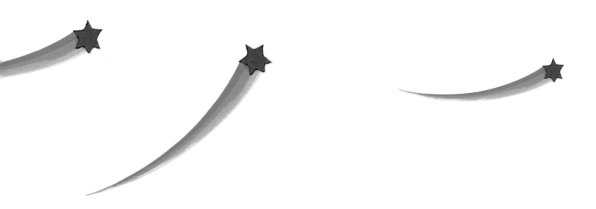

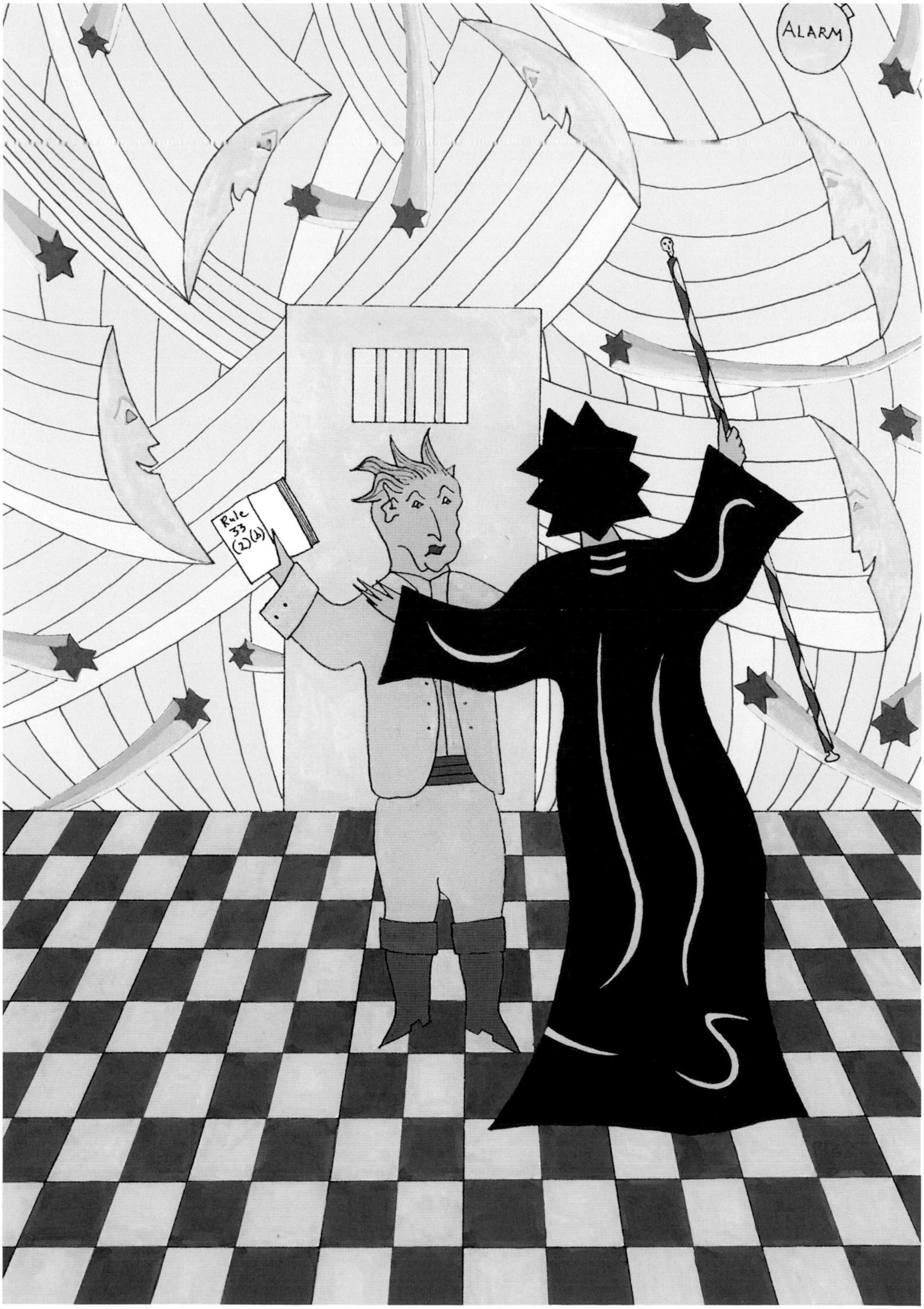
ALARM
Rule 33 (2)(b)

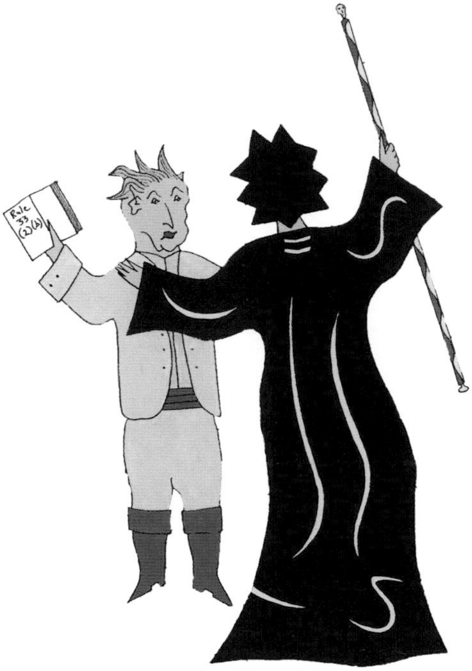
Rule
33
(2)(a)

Griselda screamed and stamped her feet. "Very well, I shall return tomorrow with the dwarves but the boys must not escape. If I pay you £50 will you chain them to the wall?"

The goblin agreed.

The boys had a dreadful night chained to the wall but just as it was getting light Scrooey-Looey awoke them, took a piece of metal out of his pocket and quickly picked the locks. The boys and rabbit hurried outside. An alarm went off.

"Lost property escaping!" screeched the goblins, grabbing their spears.

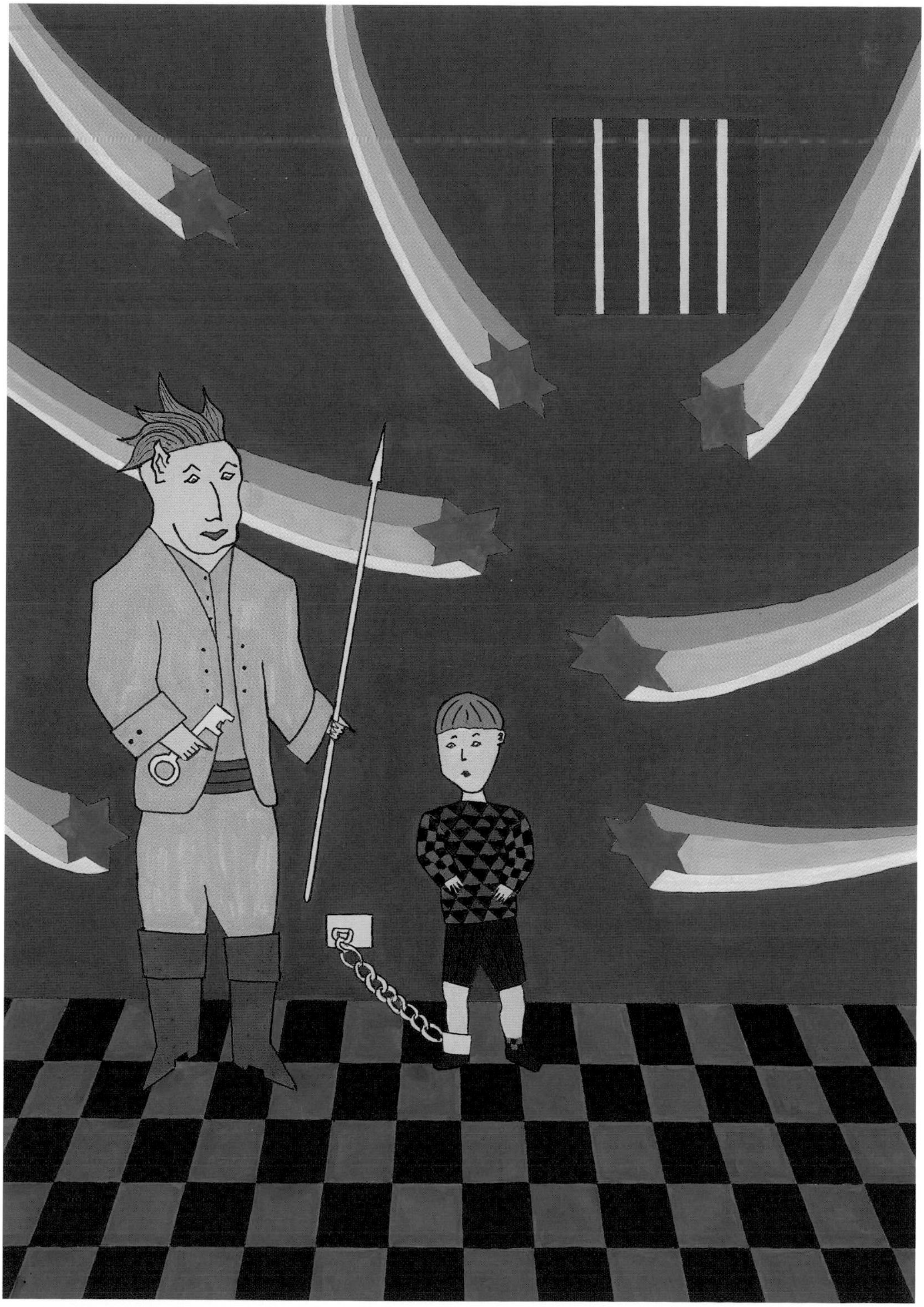

Griselda arrived with her guards, sounded her hunting horn, and bellowed "Tally ho! Off we go! Let's get them."

The goblins, Griselda and the Dim Daft Dwarves chased the boys and rabbit past the lettuce bar, through a wood, across a rocky hillside. They were only just behind them when the boys and rabbit saw a cave and hurried inside. There was a hiss and the entrance to the cave snapped shut.

"Oh dear! I think we have been eaten!" cried the boys.

When the goblins, dwarves and Griselda saw the snake, one hundred foot long, six foot high and wide, they shook with horror. Its tongue shot out, knocked the magic staff out of Griselda's hand and threw it far away: goblins, dwarves and Griselda screamed and fled.

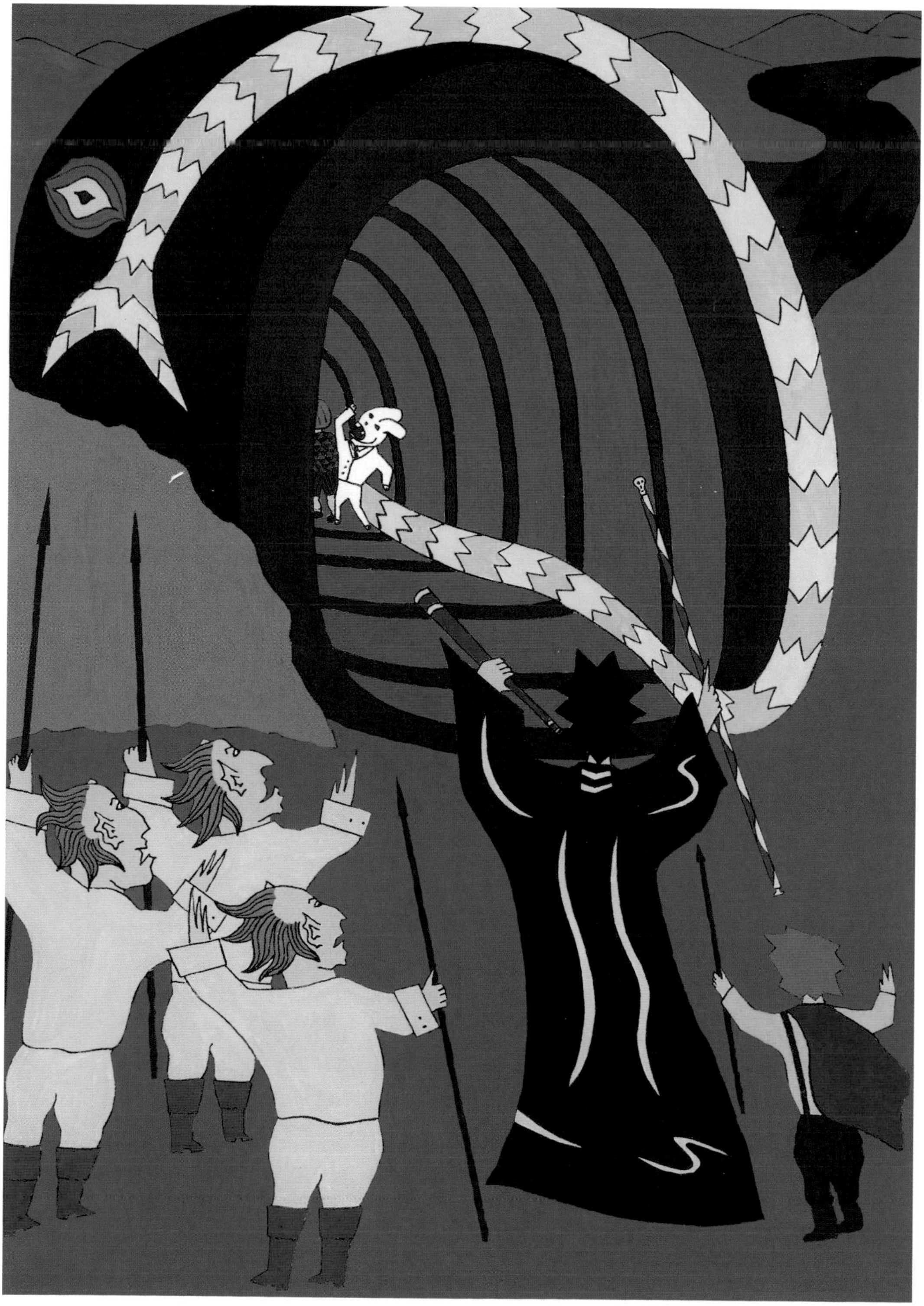

CHAPTER THREE

"What do we do now?" asked the boys. "It's not very nice being stuck inside a snake."

Scrooey-Looey took the piece of metal out of his pocket and tickled the inside of the snake.

The snake shook, wriggled, opened its mouth, hissed, "Stop it! Stop it!", then burped and sent boys and rabbit flying through the air into a nearby forest.

It was dark and creepy there.

Suddenly Alexander yelped: "Julius did you pinch me?"

"No, I did not."

"You've done it again!"

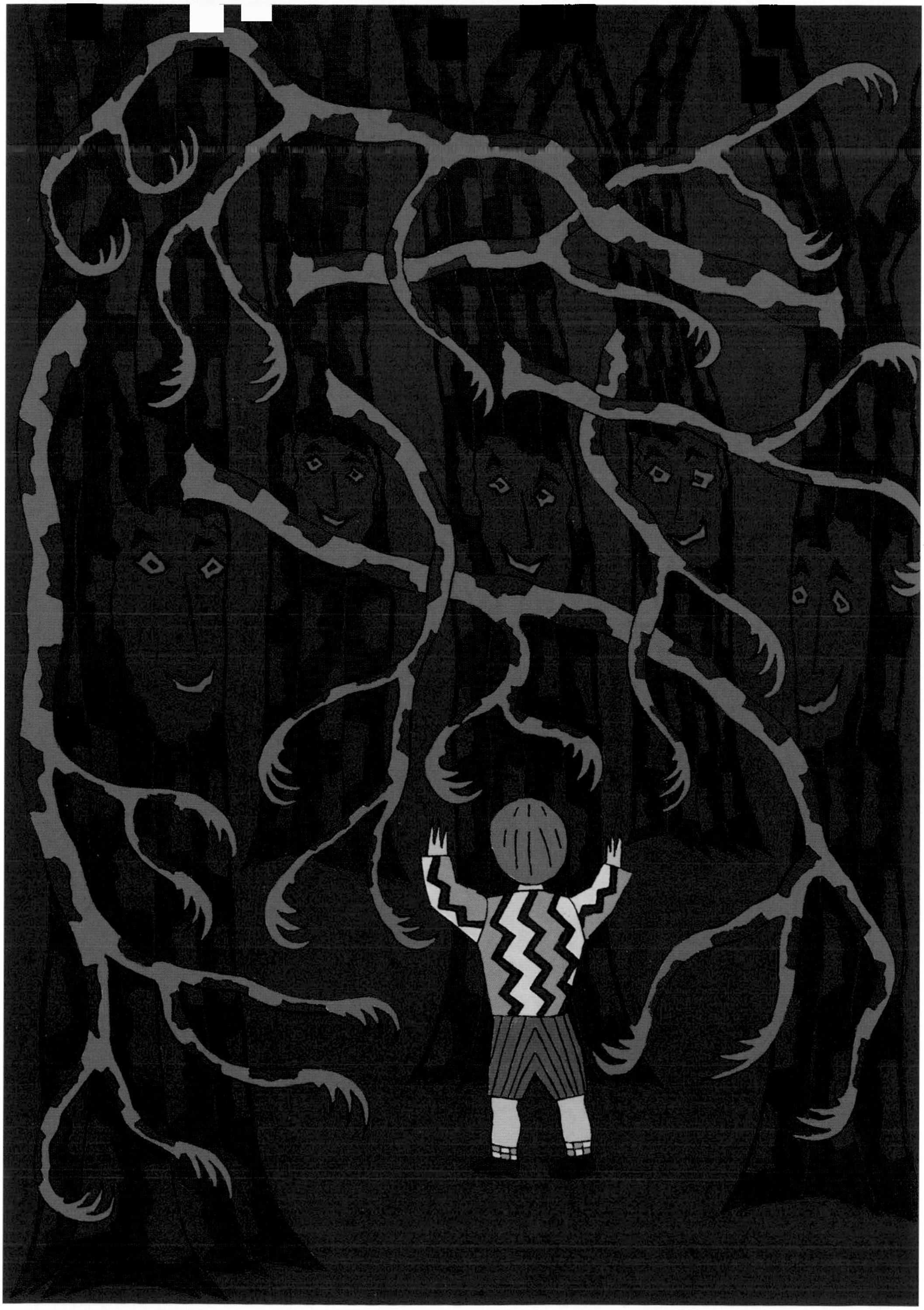

There was an evil chuckle.

"It was the branches of that tree," cried Benjamin.

The tree trunk had green eyes and a leering mouth. It chuckled again as it stretched out a twiggy branch and pinched Alexander hard.

"It's creeping nearer!" screamed Benjamin in horror.

"Oh help!" cried Scrooey-Looey, shaking like a jelly.

All around the boys and rabbit were trees with evil eyes and leering mouths. They were slowly edging closer, bending down their twiggy branches and twiggy fingers to pinch the boys and rabbit hard.

"Run, run, run!" cried Julius, taking Benjamin and Scrooey-Looey by the hand.

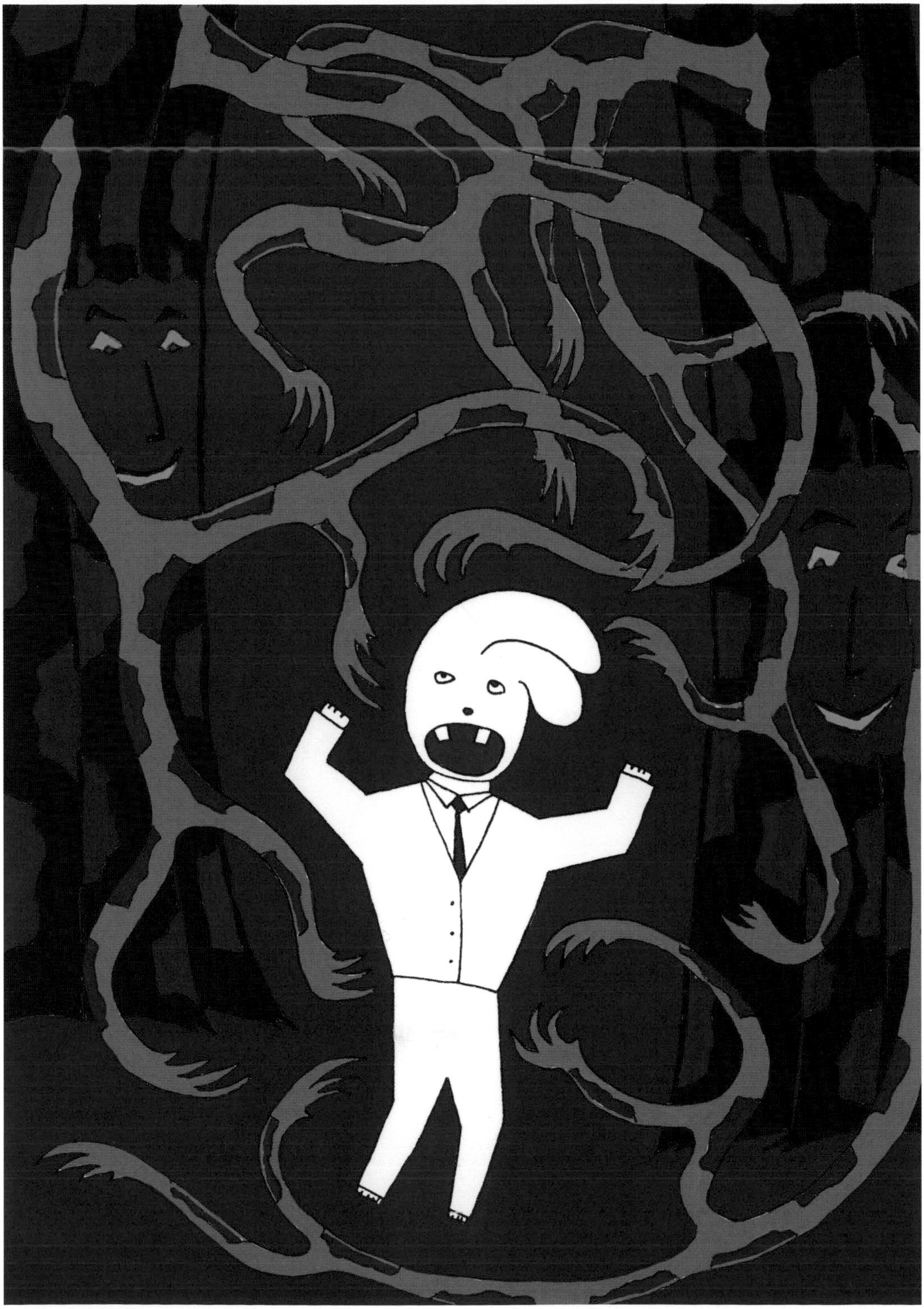

The boys and rabbit ran and ran when, from between the trees, there appeared Globerous Ghosts.

Globerous Ghosts are the fattest, ooziest ghosts that have ever lived. A single touch from their arms will turn a boy (or rabbit) into a ghostly glob.

In front of the boys and rabbit stretched a deep, black pond. Behind them, floating ever nearer, came the Globerous Ghosts with outstretched arms.

"We are trapped!" screamed Alexander.

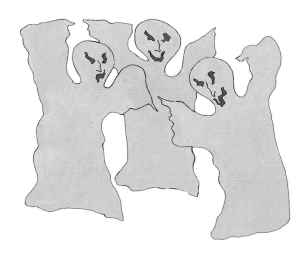

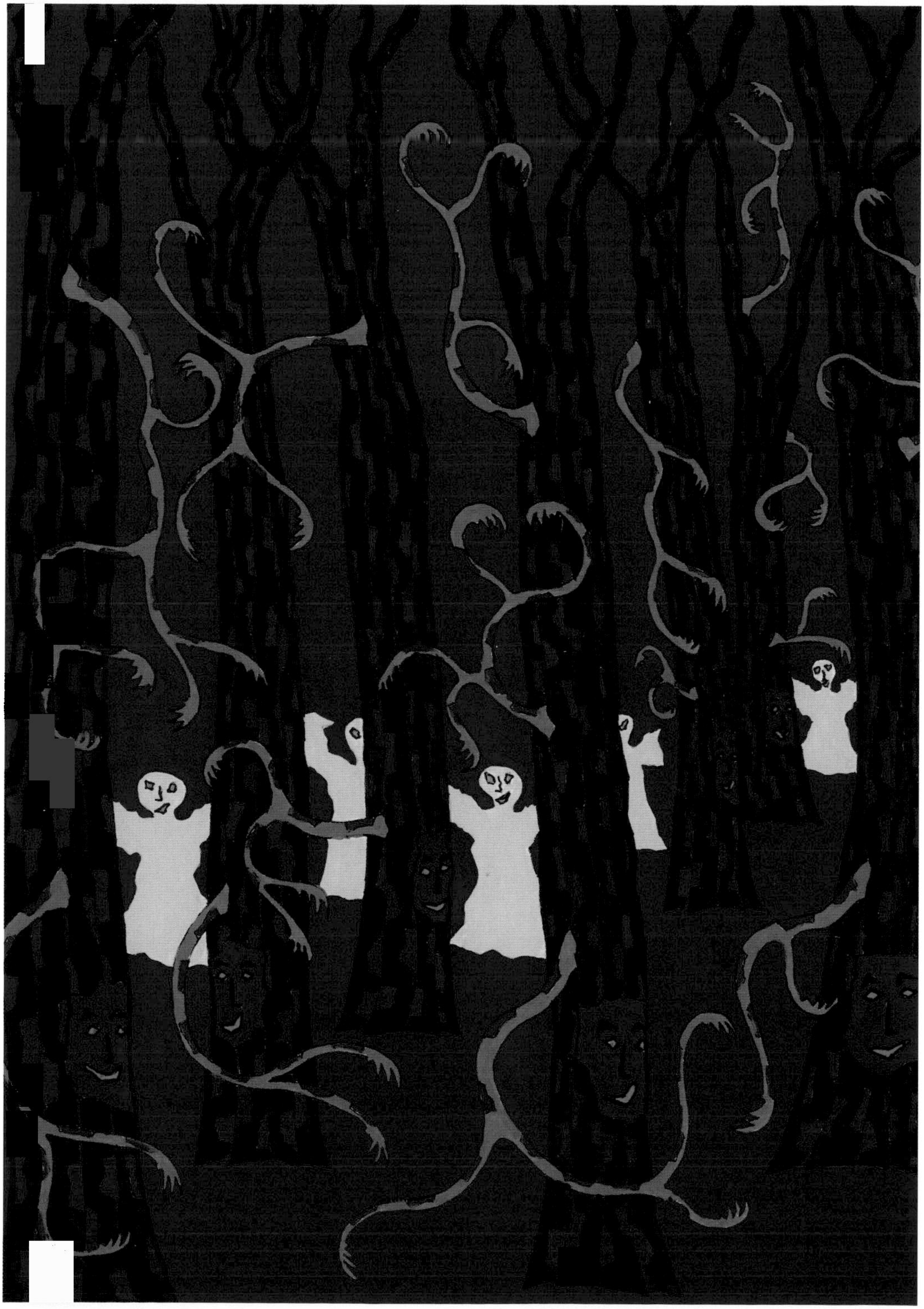

The boys and the rabbit huddled together, quaking with fear. The Globerous Ghosts had nearly got them when from the pond there came a glug, glug, glug.

It was the Ducky Rocky.

The Ducky Rocky's ancestors had grown a shell of rock as protection from hunters' guns, but his shell had become so heavy that the Ducky Rocky could not fly or float. He lived upon the bottom of the pond coming up once or twice a day for air. To swim to the surface was terribly hard work.

With great splashing the Ducky Rocky emerged, gasped for air and cried, "Stick out your tongues," then sank to the bottom of the pond.

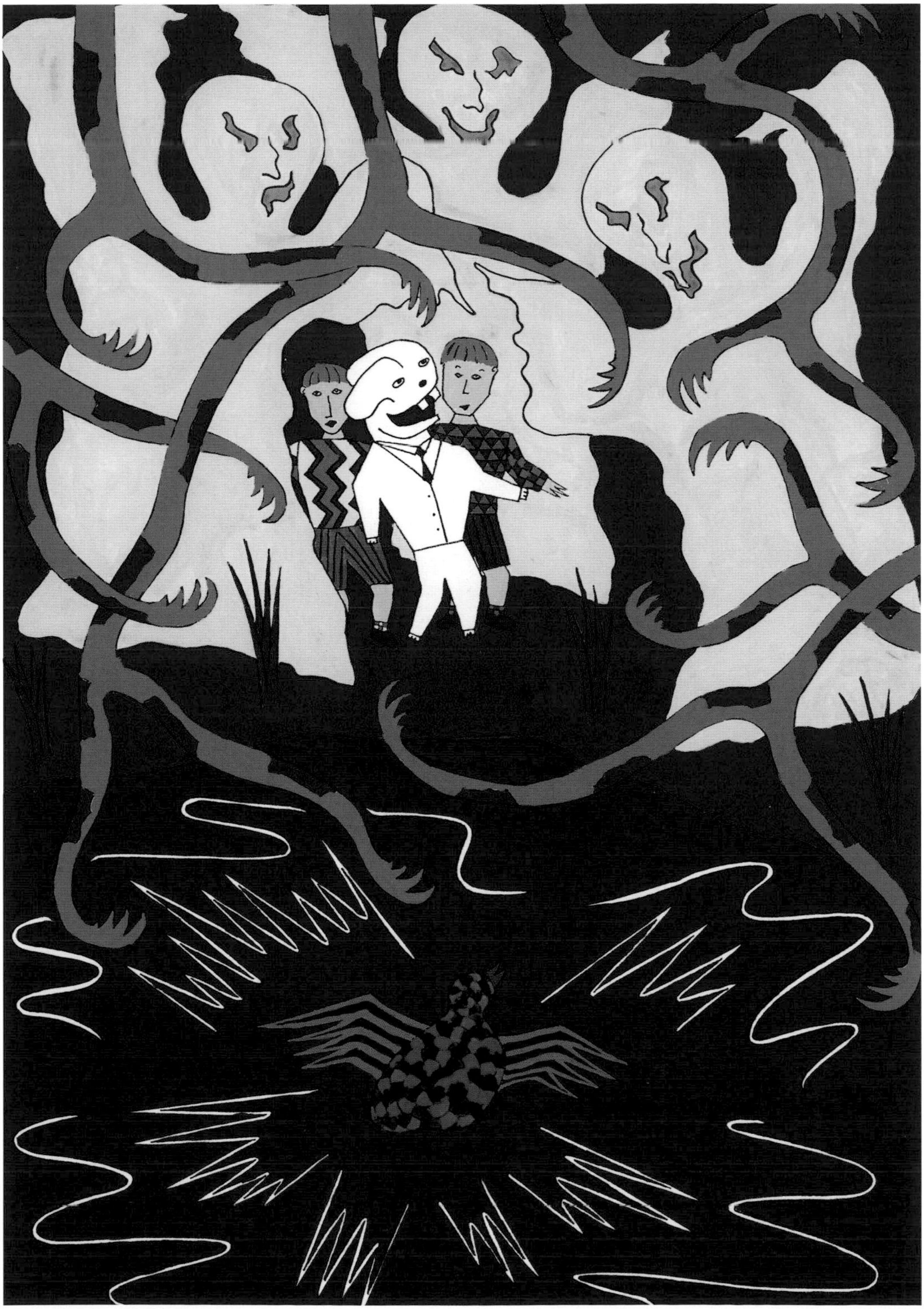

The boys stuck out their tongues.

The one thing Globerous Ghosts cannot stand is boys who stick their tongues out. As soon as they saw the boys sticking out their tongues the Globerous Ghosts exploded into a thousand ghostly globs which splattered all around the forest.

"That was a lucky escape," gasped the boys, putting in their tongues.

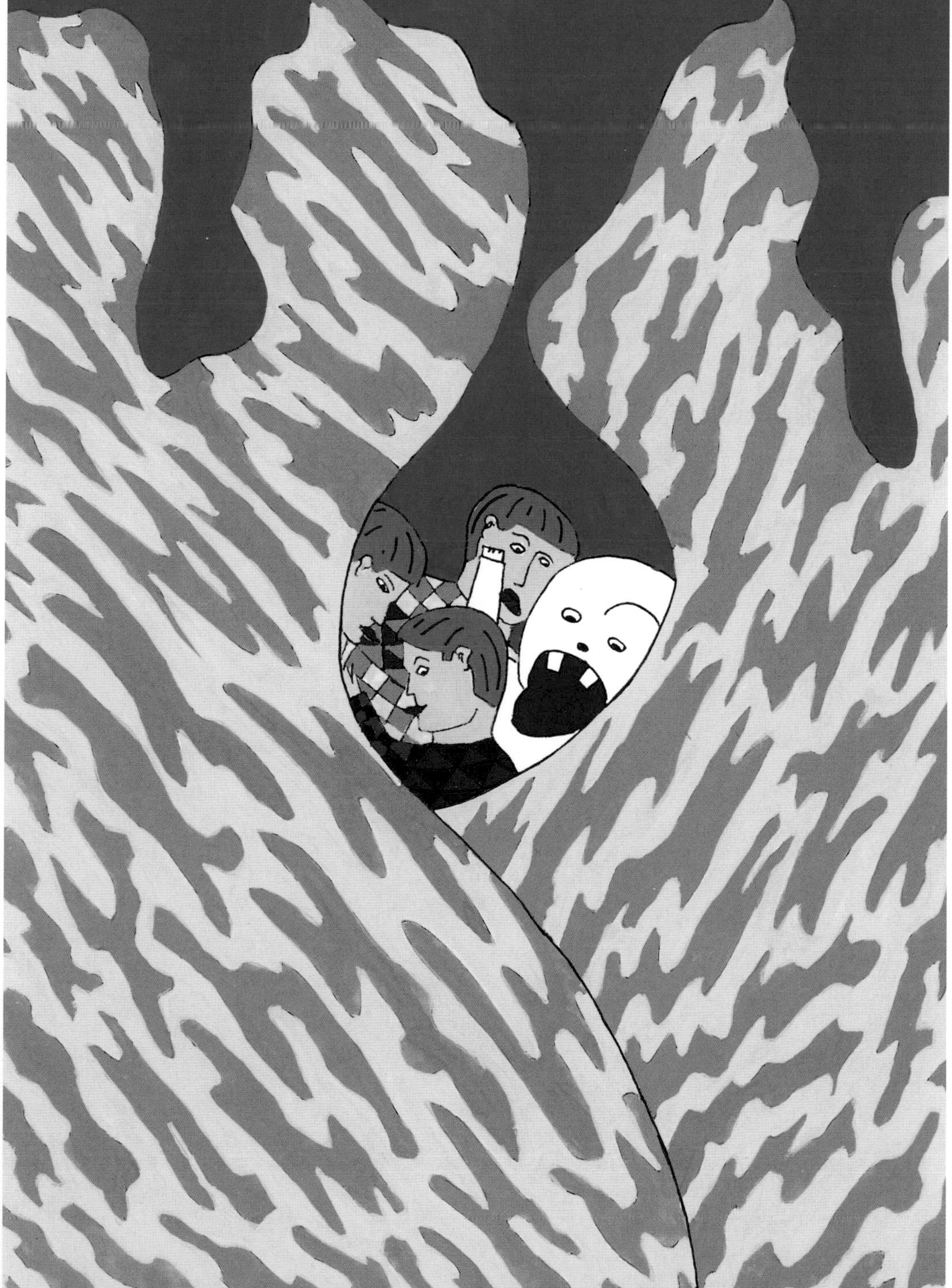

The boys and rabbit had hardly stopped shaking when from between the trees there appeared Mystic Mummies. Mystic Mummies are the most evil mummies that have ever lived. A single touch from their arms will turn a boy (or rabbit) into a pile of dust.

The boys and rabbit huddled together, quaking with fear. The Mystic Mummies had nearly got them when from the pond there came a glug, glug, glug.

"Come on, Ducky Rocky. Come on! Come on! Tell us what to do," cried the boys, as the Mystic Mummies stretched out their arms to turn them into dust.

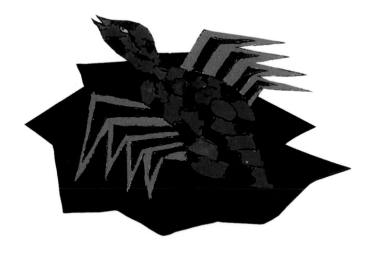

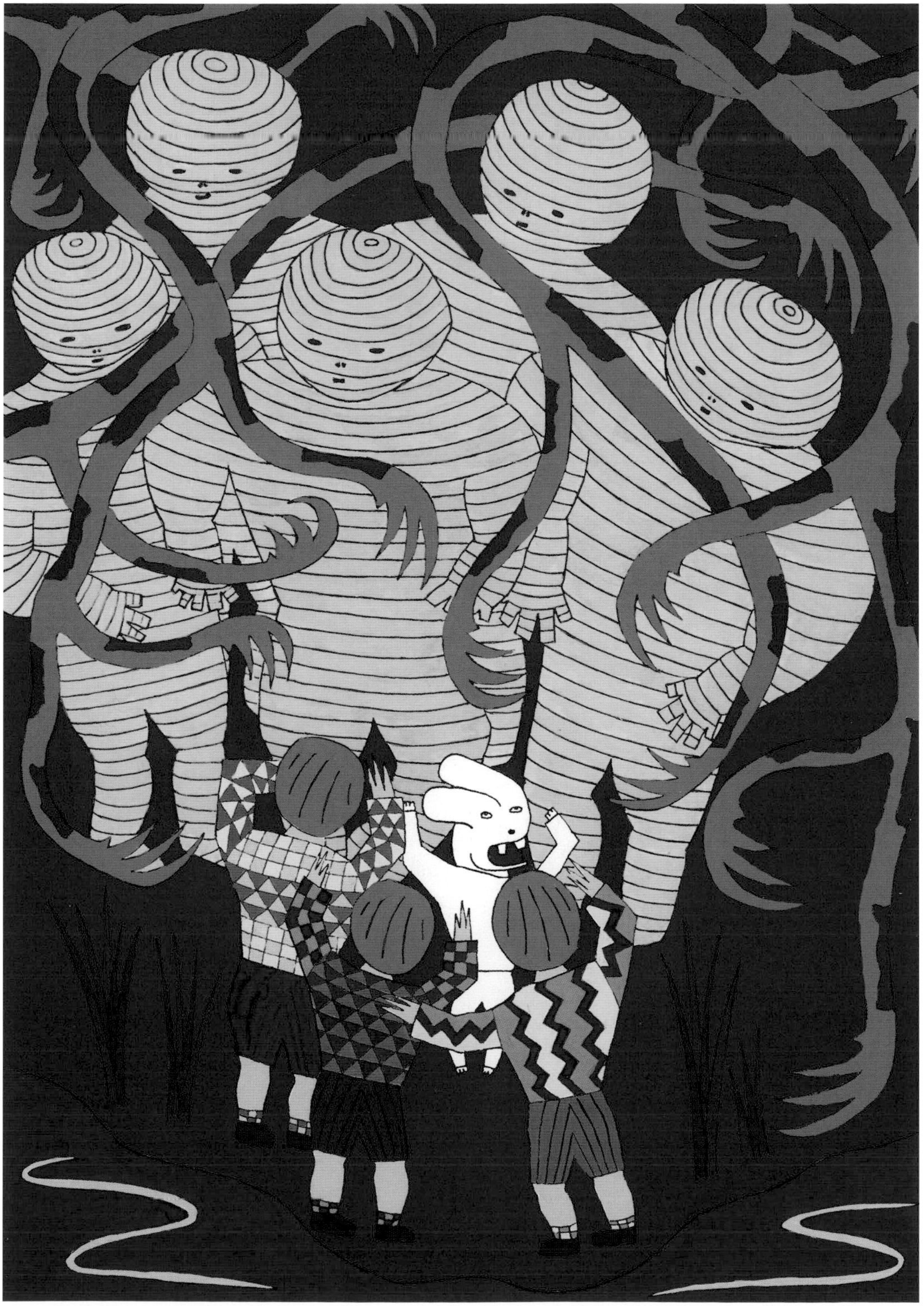

The Ducky Rocky was swimming as hard as he could. He reached the surface, gasped for air, cried, "Pick your noses," then sank to the bottom of the pond.

The boys picked their noses. The one thing Mystic Mummies (like other mummies) cannot stand is boys who pick their noses. As soon as they saw the boys picking their noses they screamed, "Germs! Germs!" Their bandages unravelled and blew away in the wind. Their innards turned to dust.

"Lucky escape," murmured the boys, taking their fingers out of their noses.

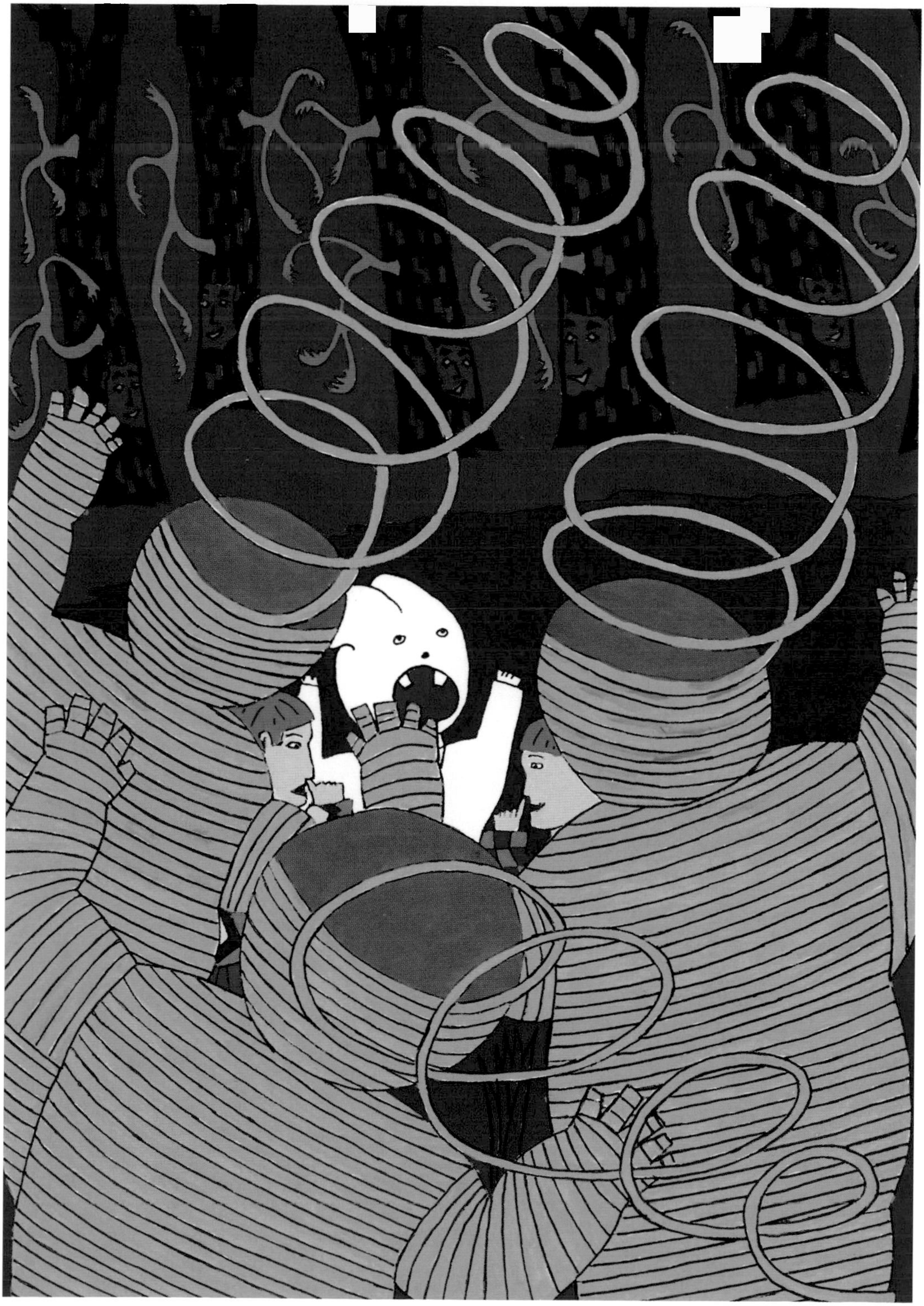

The boys and rabbit had not stopped shaking when from between the trees there appeared Venomous Vampires, dressed in full evening dress with white bow-ties and long-tailed coats, speaking in snooty voices: "Boys! Come here, boys. We only want your blood." One bite from their fangs would drain the blood out of the body of a boy or rabbit.

The boys and rabbit huddled together, trembling with fear. The Venomous Vampires were taking napkins from their pockets (they did not want to splatter blood over their clothes) when from the pond there came a glug, glug, glug.

"Come on, Ducky Rocky. Come on! Come on! Tell us what to do," cried the boys, as the Venomous Vampires opened their mouths and licked their fangs.

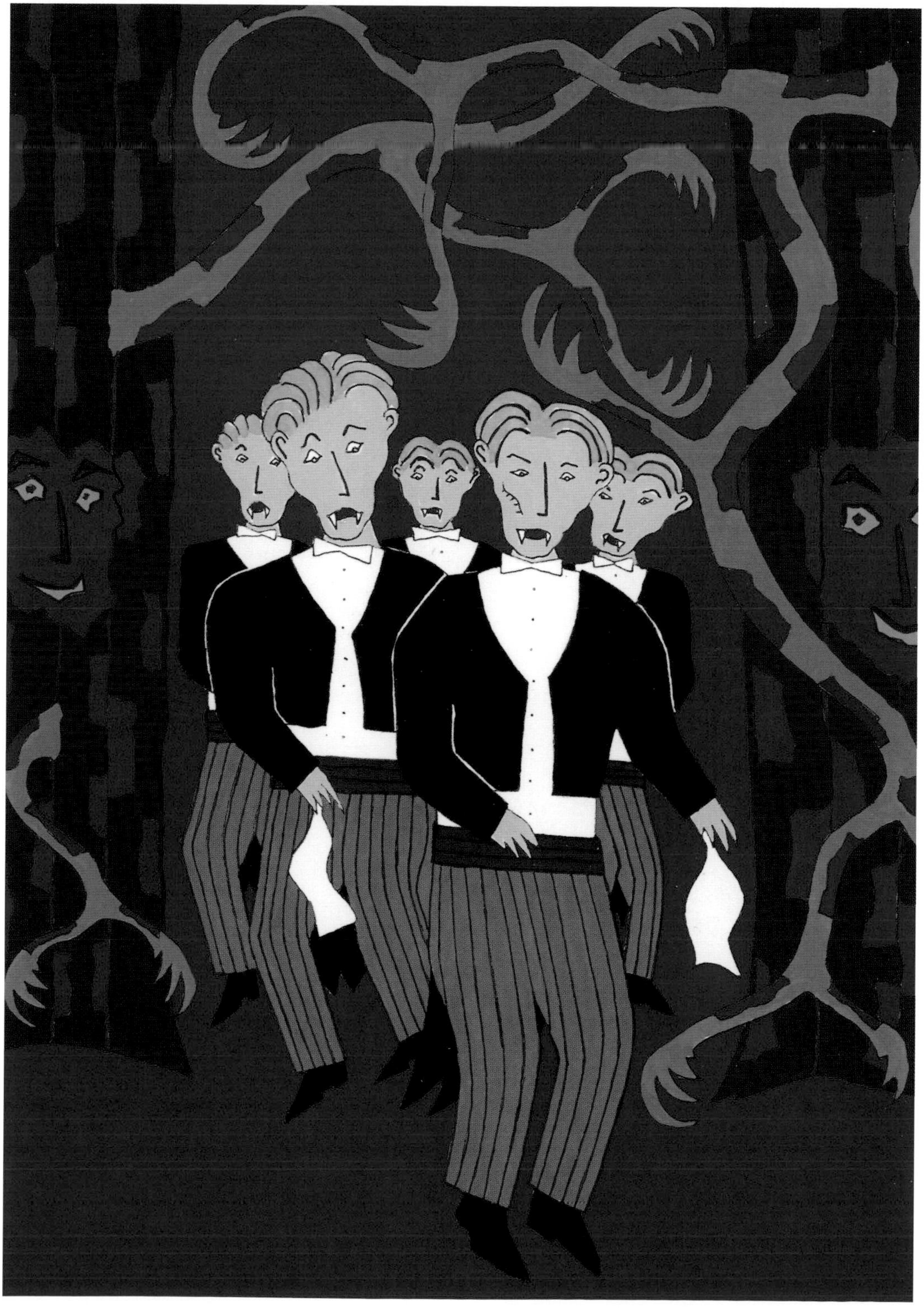

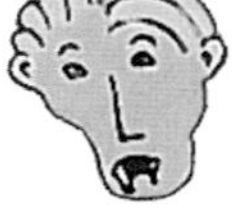
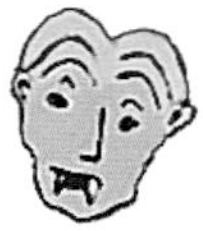
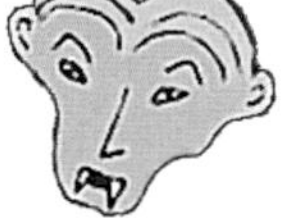

The Ducky Rocky normally swam to the surface once or twice a day. He was almost exhausted. He reached the surface, gasped for air, cried, "Muddy hands!" before sinking once more to the bottom of the pond.

Quickly the boys bent down, stuck their hands in the muddy ground and held them out towards the Venomous Vampires. The Venomous Vampires screamed, "Oh no! Not the muddy hands!" as their heads shot off and bounced away and their bodies ran off to the dry cleaners.

"What luck," gasped the boys wiping their hands on their pullovers.

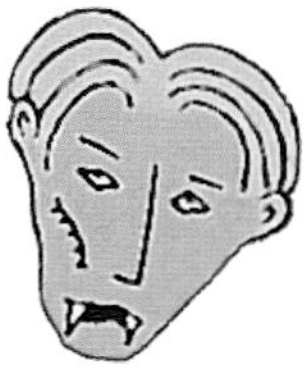
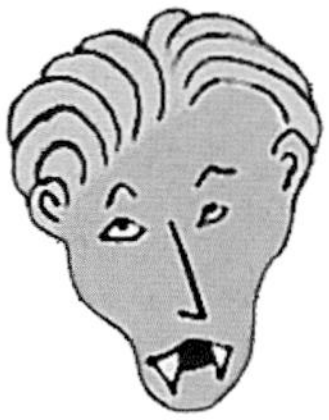

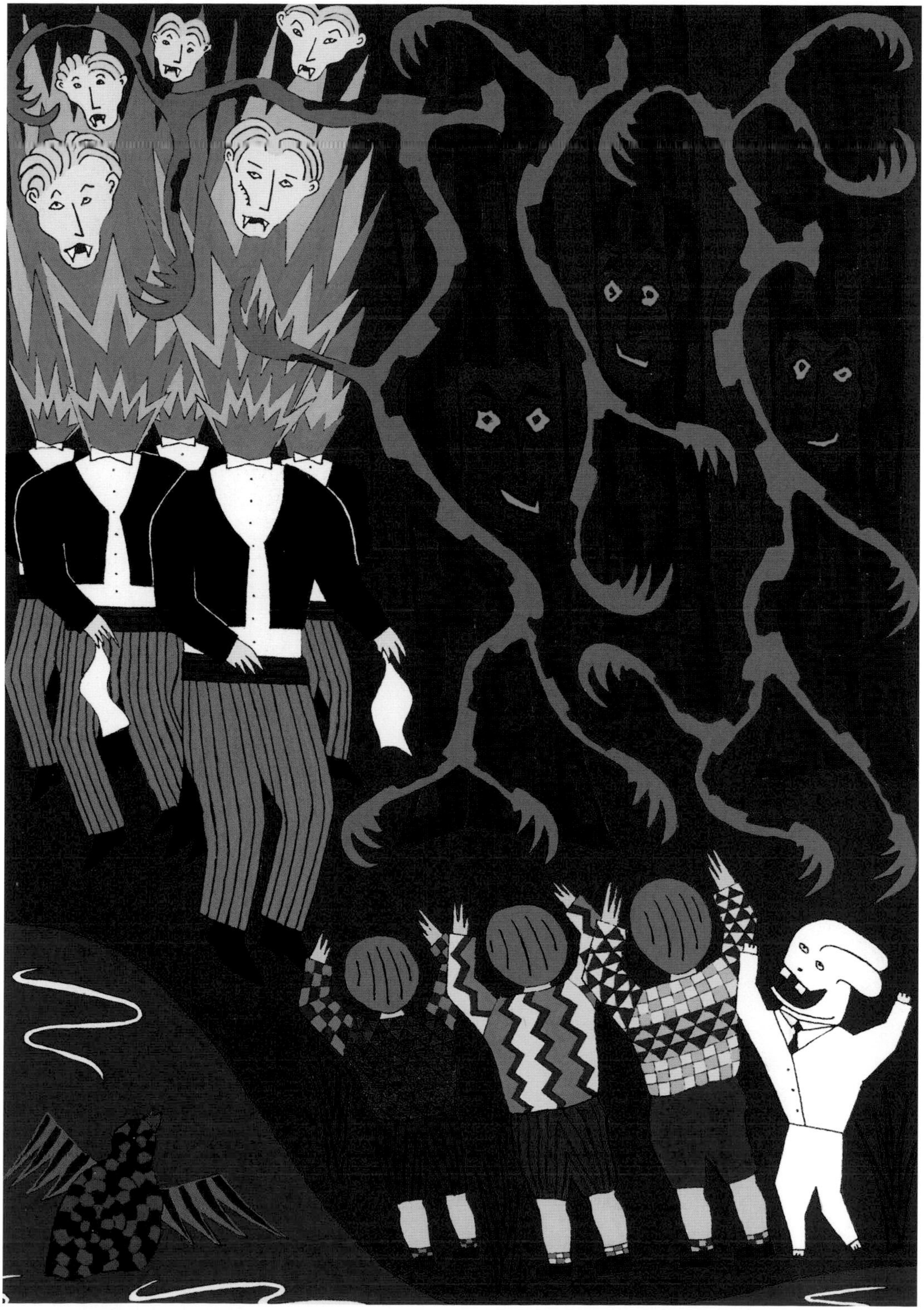

The boys and rabbit were still trembling when from between the trees there appeared Scary Scots dressed in kilts and playing bagpipes. The boys and rabbit screamed in horror. Globerous Ghosts are bad, Mystic Mummies very bad, Venomous Vampires very, very bad, but Scary Scots with bagpipes are even worse. Five minutes of that sound and a boy (or rabbit) will explode.

The five minutes were almost up when from the pond there came a glug, glug, glug.

"Come on, Ducky Rocky. Come on! Come on! Tell us what to do," cried the boys, as the bagpipes wheezed and groaned and filled their ears with deadly sound.

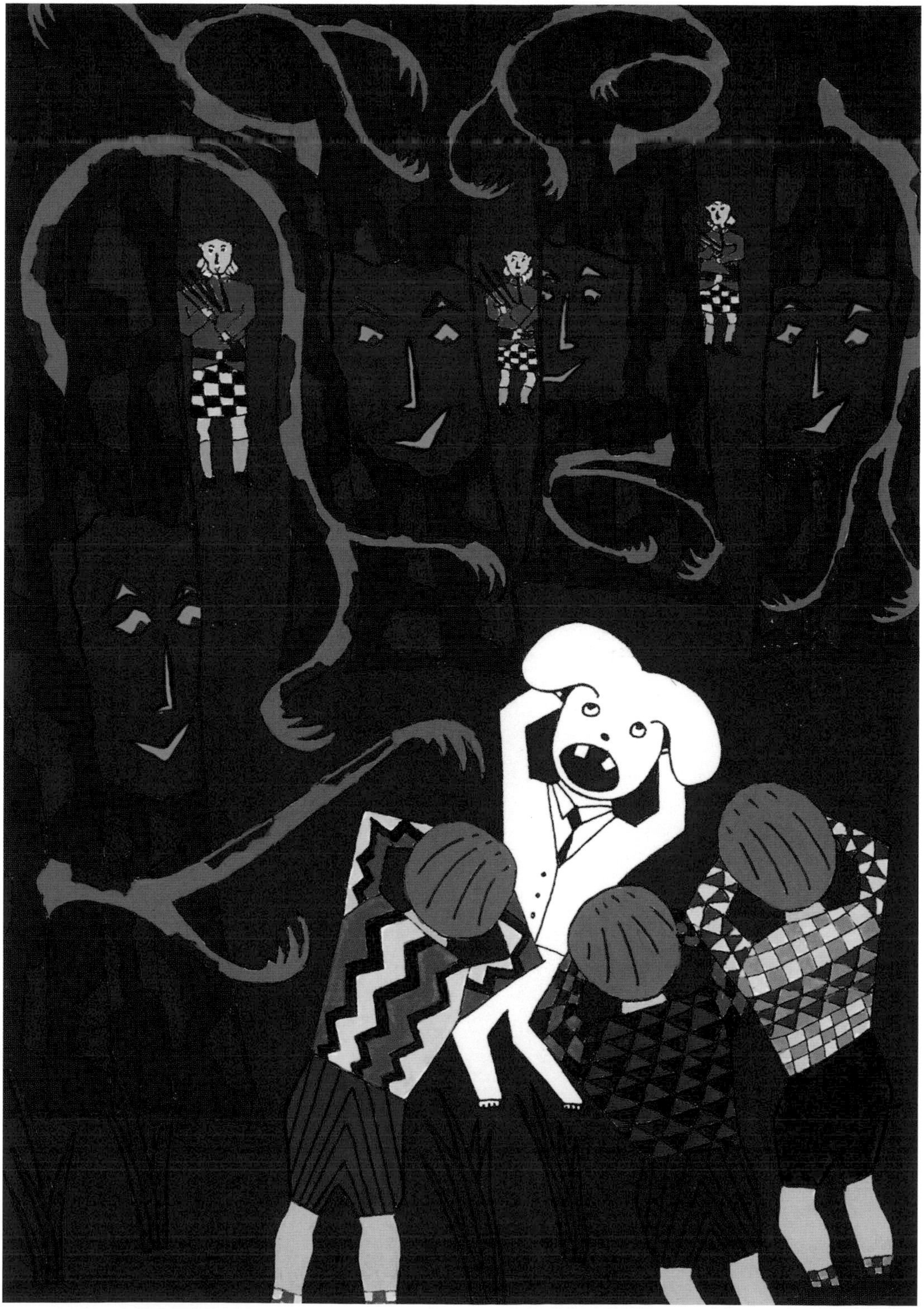

The Ducky Rocky swam as hard as he could, reached the surface, but before he could speak, sank to the bottom: he was exhausted.

"We've had it," cried the boys and rabbit in despair.

But at that moment two Hero Hedgehogs ran out of the bushes (they should have been Horrid Hedgehogs but the spell had gone wrong). They saluted smartly, and stuck their bottoms in the air facing the Scary Scots.

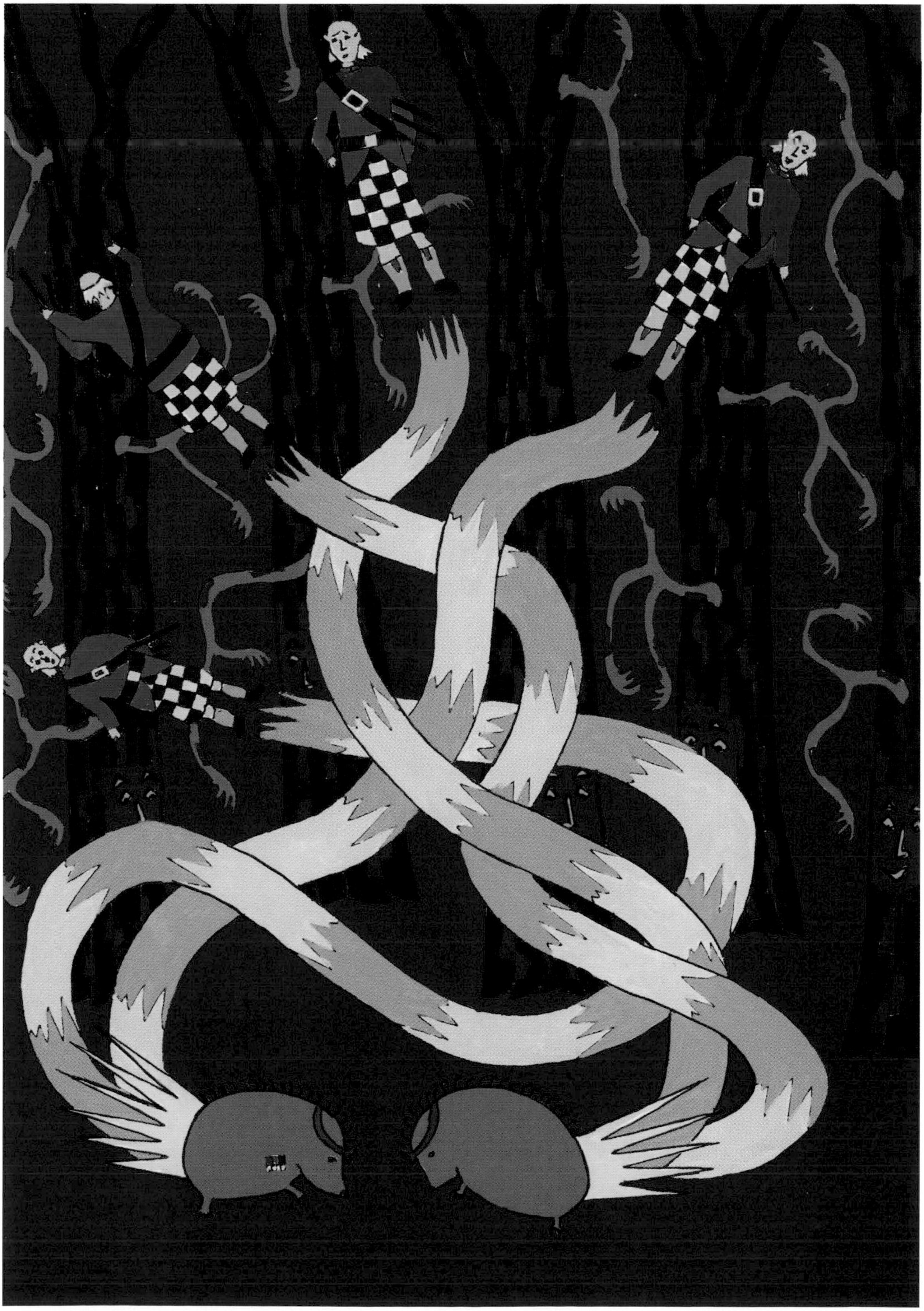

With very rude sounds, spines shot out of the bottoms of the Hero Hedgehogs. The spines punctured the bagpipes sending Scary Scots all over the forest like burst balloons. The boys and Scrooey-Looey cheered and cheered.

The Hero Hedgehogs got up and saluted smartly. They had run out of ammunition: their bottoms were bare. They ran off into the forest to reload.

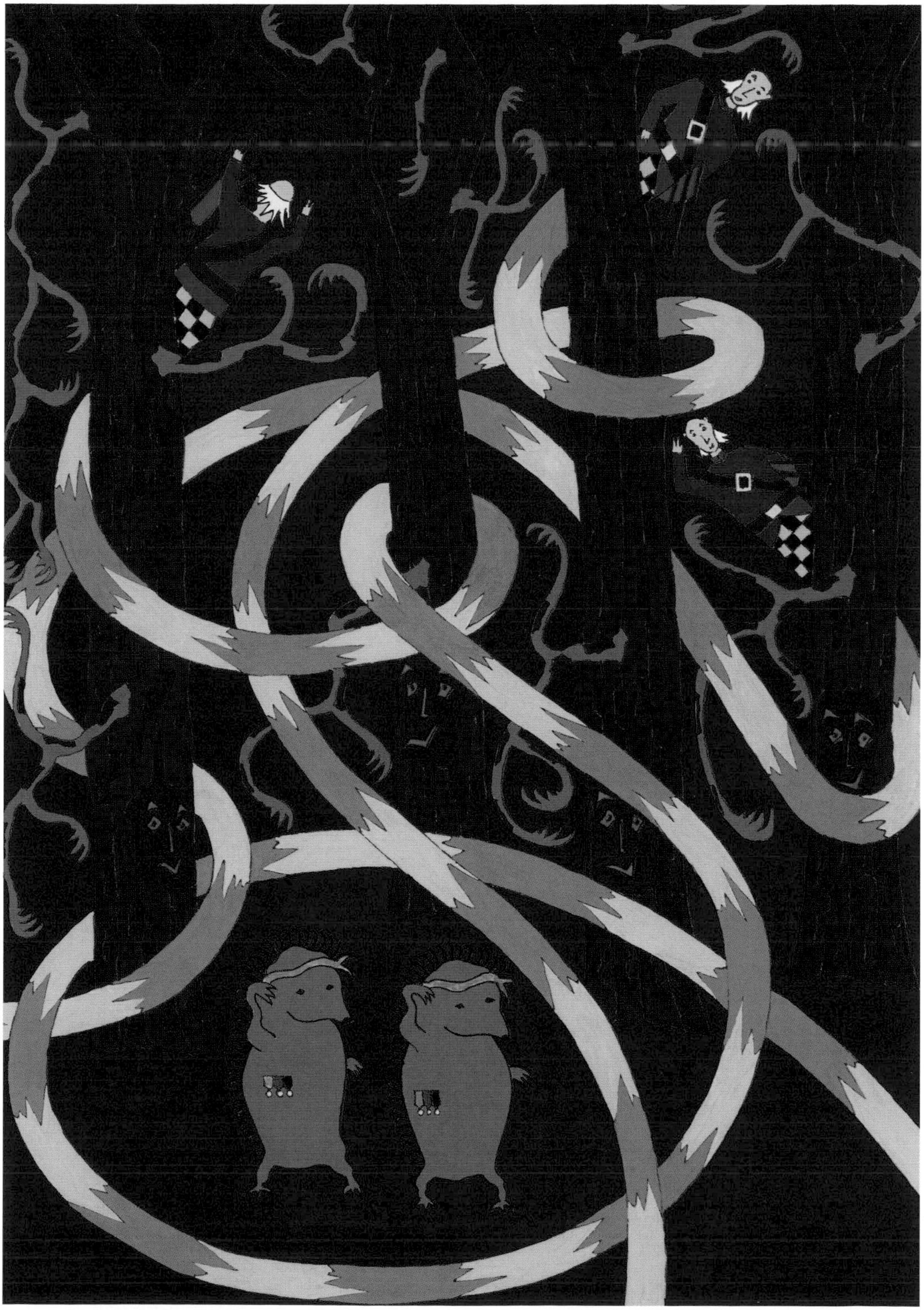

As soon as the Hero Hedgehogs had disappeared, a flapping noise filled the air. The boys looked up in despair as huge butterflies with sickly pink wings flew down upon them.

The Bilious Butterflies seized the boys and rabbit and carried them struggling to a gnarled old man in a glade in the middle of the forest.

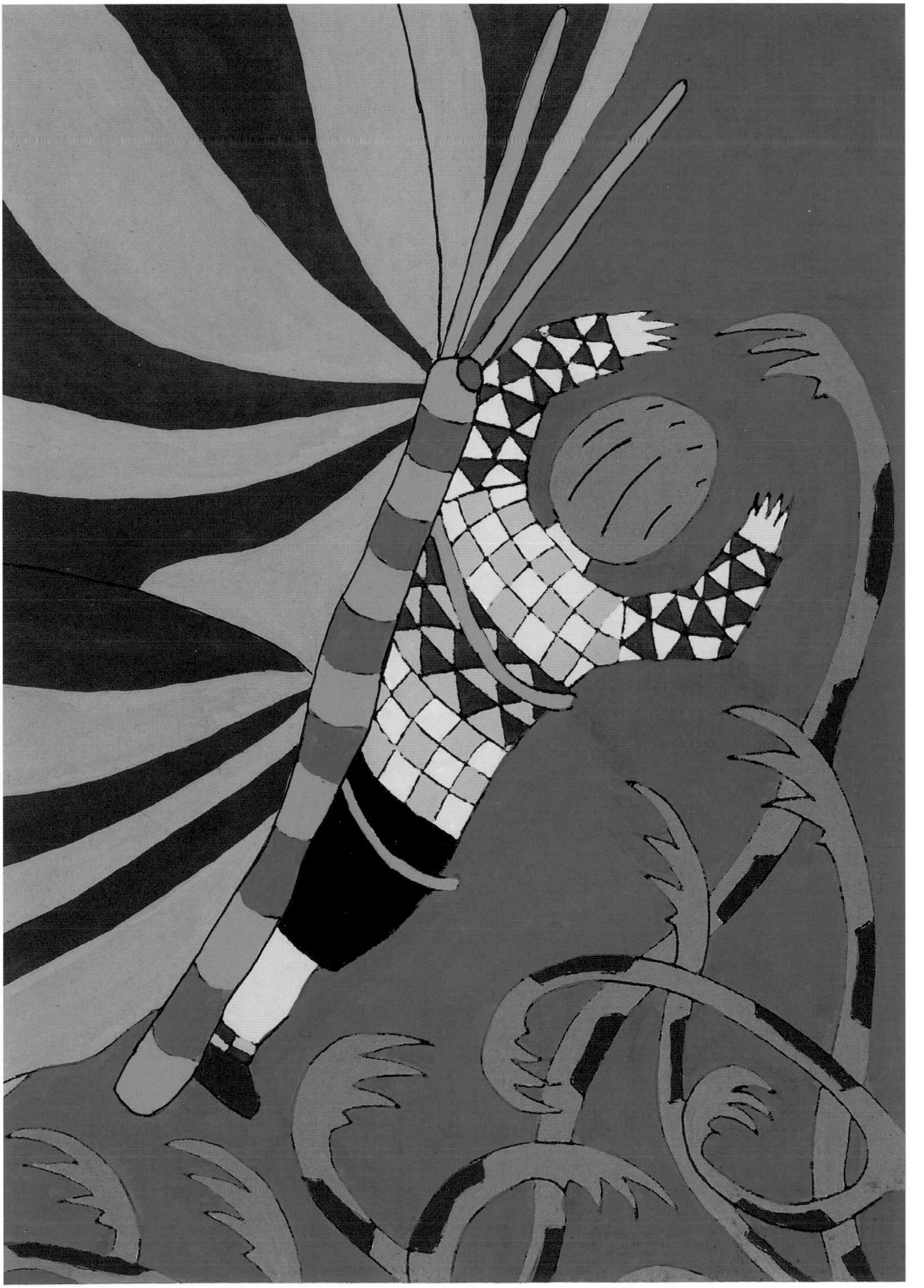

CHAPTER FOUR

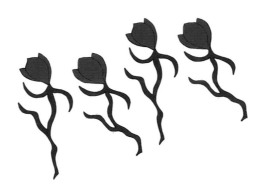

The Bilious Butterflies dropped the boys and rabbit at the feet of the Gnarled Old Man. He was very angry.

"You have destroyed my pets," snarled the Gnarled Old Man. "My Globerous Ghosts are in globs all over the forest. My Mystic Mummies have unravelled. The heads of my Venomous Vampires are bouncing around like footballs - their bodies have gone to the dry cleaners. My Scary Scots are stuck at the top of trees."

"Hip, hip, hooray!" cried the boys.

"Quiet!" screamed the Gnarled Old Man. "You will not escape. You will become my pets." The boys and rabbit quaked with fear. "Now let me see. I am up to Z. You will be Zany Zombies."

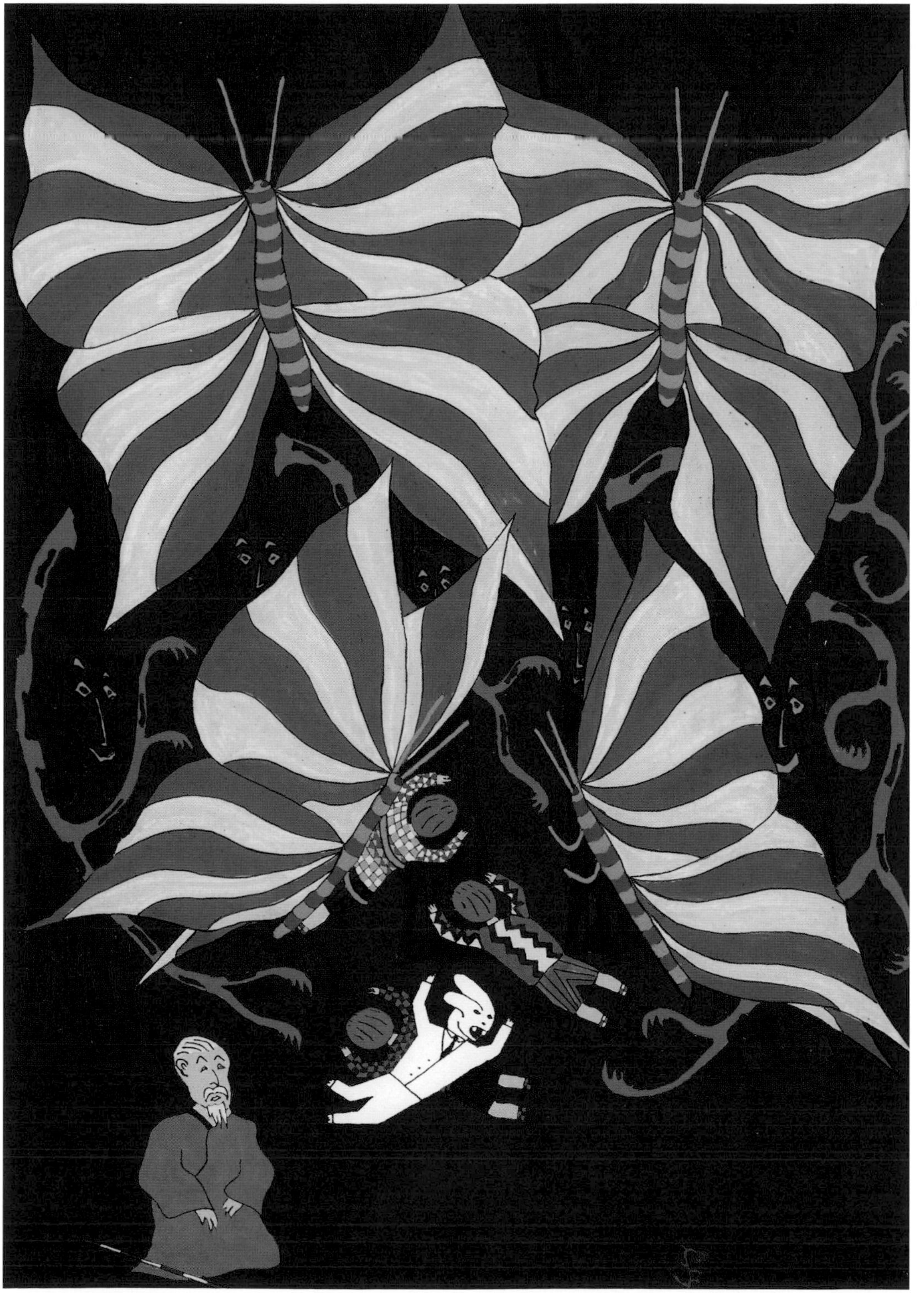

"What are Zany Zombies?" asked the boys in dread.

"The living dead. They have faces of green and purple stripes. Quite attractive if you like that sort of thing."

The boys and Scrooey-Looey did not. "Couldn't we stay as we are?"

"Definitely not."

As the Gnarled Old Man turned away and reached for his magic staff he did not notice four Precious Plants (they should have been Putrid Plants but the spell had gone wrong) creep up behind the boys and rabbit and jump into their pockets.

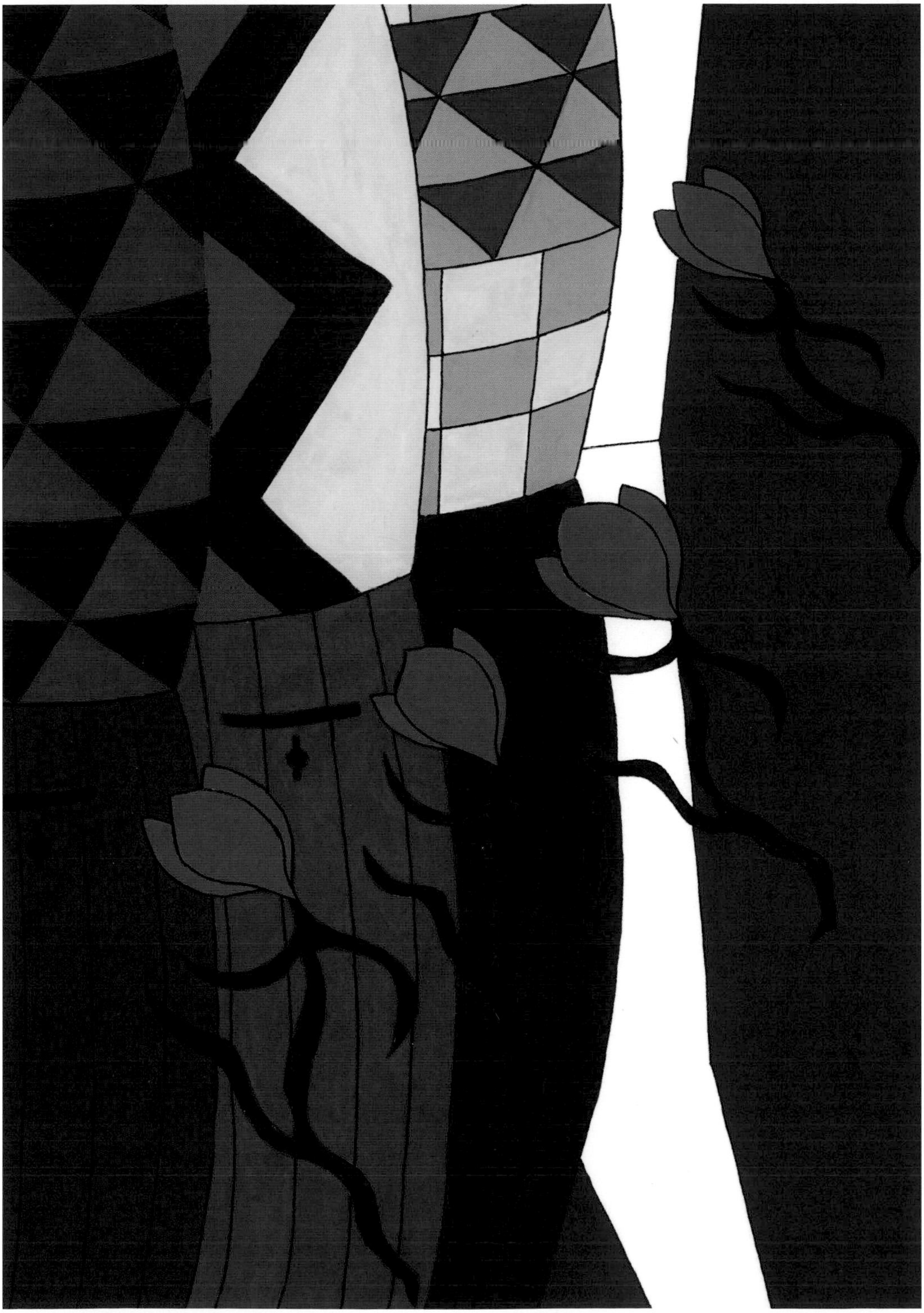

The Gnarled Old Man gave an evil laugh. "I shall enjoy having Zany Zombies creeping through the forest. They will add a little colour."

He pointed his magic staff at the boys and rabbit and uttered a curse but the little plants reversed the magic: the Gnarled Old Man became a Zany Zombie and with a scream of fury disappeared into the forest to find the antidote.

"That was a bit of luck," exclaimed the boys. "If only we could get out of this forest."

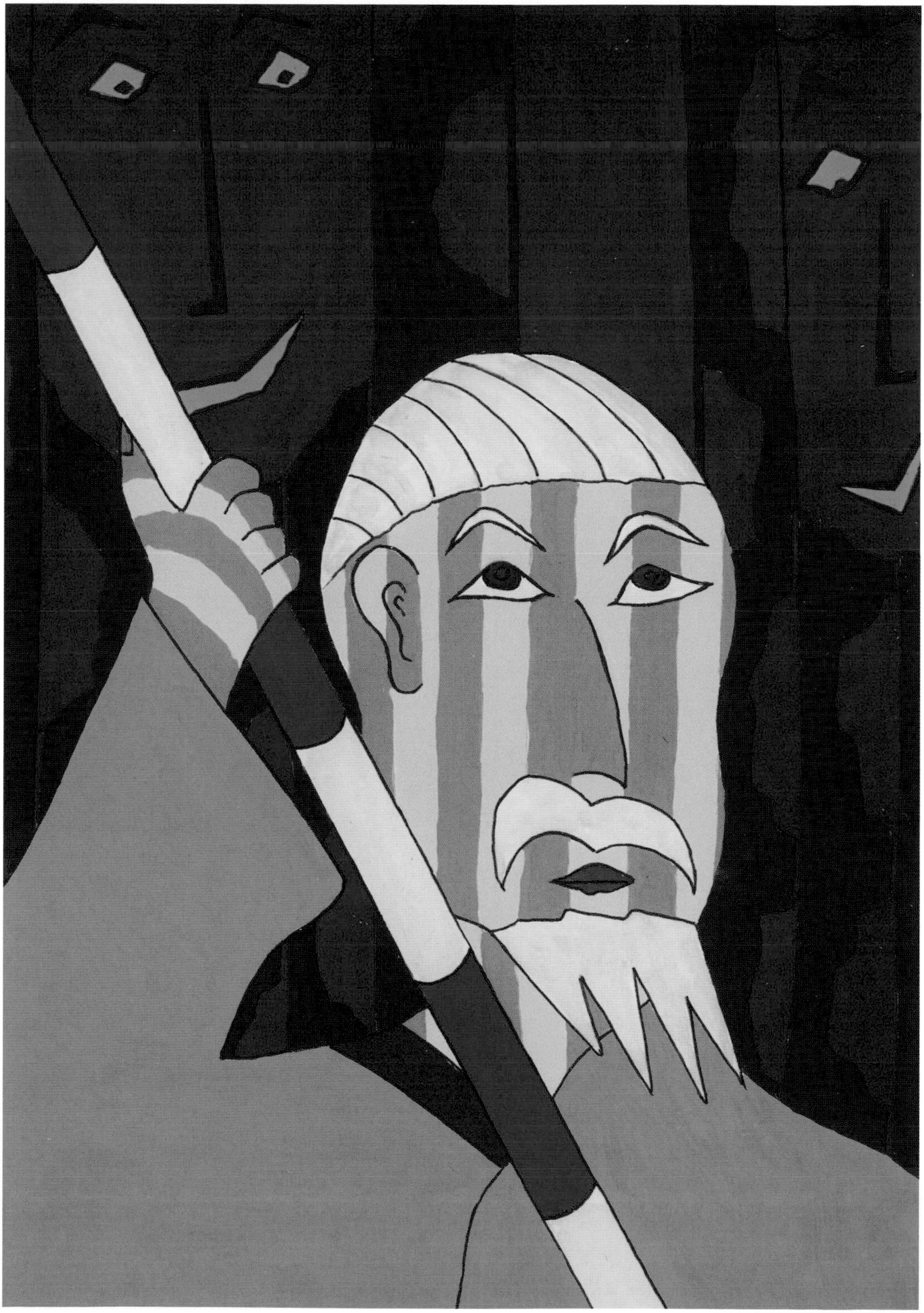

At that moment four Racing Racoons came to the rescue (they should have been Rancid Racoons but the spell had gone wrong).

The Racing Racoons rode motorbikes through the forest, revving the engines hard, speeding between the trees.

"Get up behind us," they cried. "Once we were boys like you. We hate that cruel old man. We are here to rescue you."

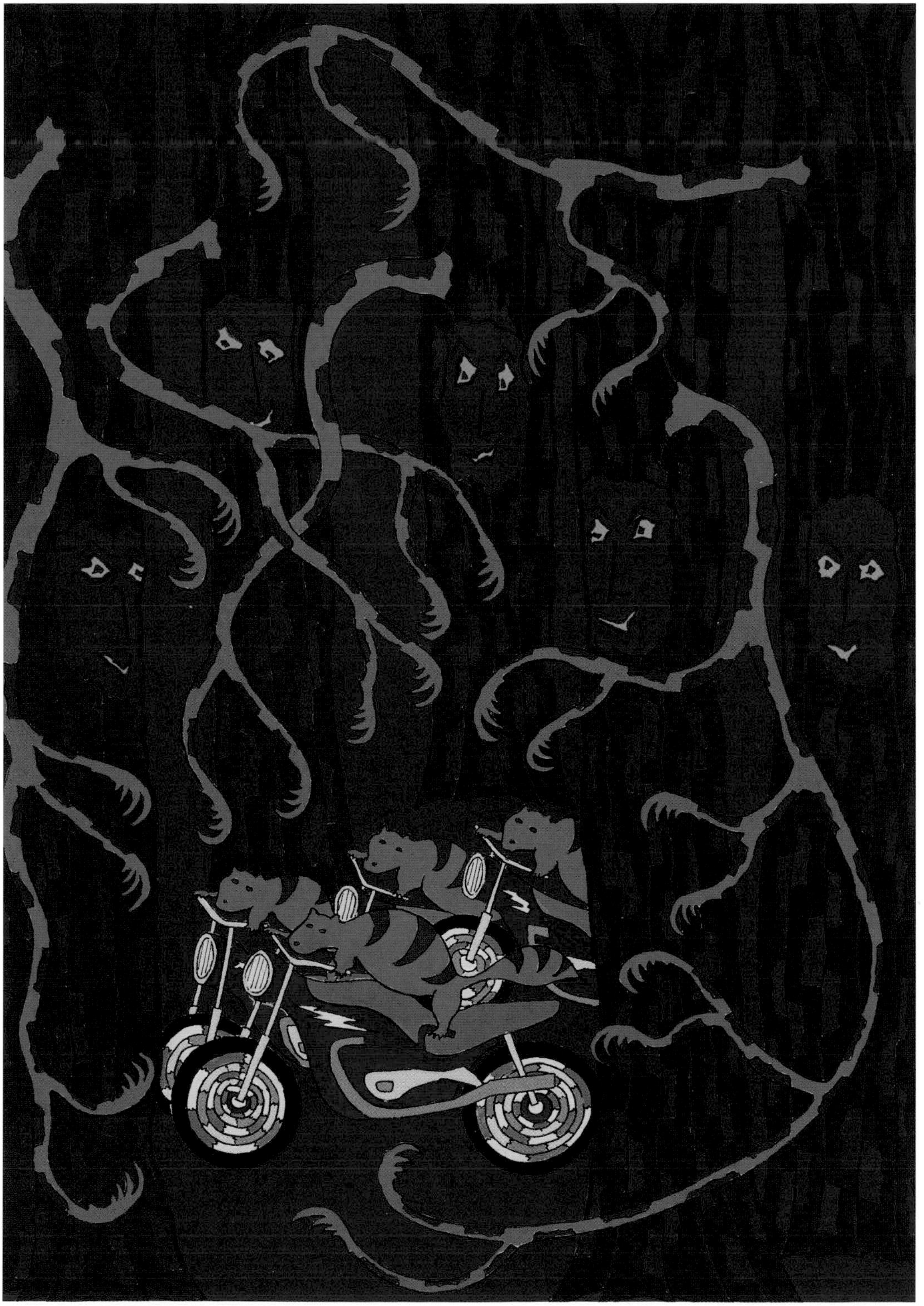

The Racing Racoons sped between the trunks of the trees, which tried to bend down to catch the boys and rabbit but were too stiff and slow.

"Way to go!" shouted the boys, punching their fists in the air.

The Racing Racoons left their passengers just outside the forest and roared off.

The boys and Scrooey-Looey lay down in the grass.

Scrooey-Looey wiped a paw across his brow and moaned, "I have a slight headache. I led a fairly quiet life before I met you lot."

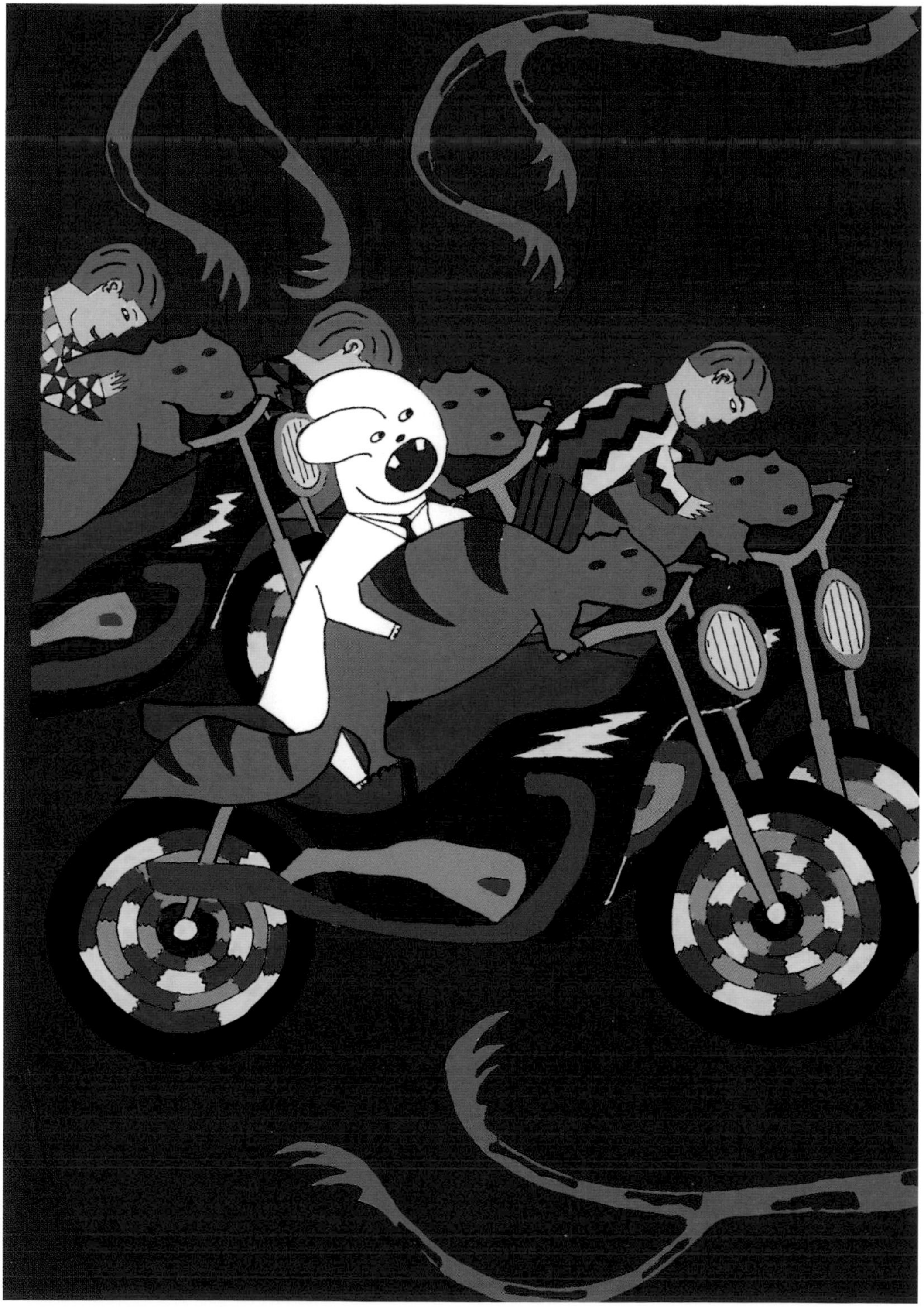

Chapter Five

Goblins pounced with spears and net. They threw Scrooey-Looey into a nearby bush, chained the boys in the back of their van and drove to the market.

"Lot Number 55," cried the Head Goblin who was in charge of the auction. "Boys. Three boys. Almost new. Mint condition. Going cheap."

The boys were on the platform with the other merchandise. Anxiously they strained their necks to see who would bid for them. In the back row was a fat lady, Miss Poggenpop, with her friend, Miss Clack. They were cooks at the castle who needed boys to do the washing up. In front of them was a fat man with a rhino whip, wanting slaves for his plantation.

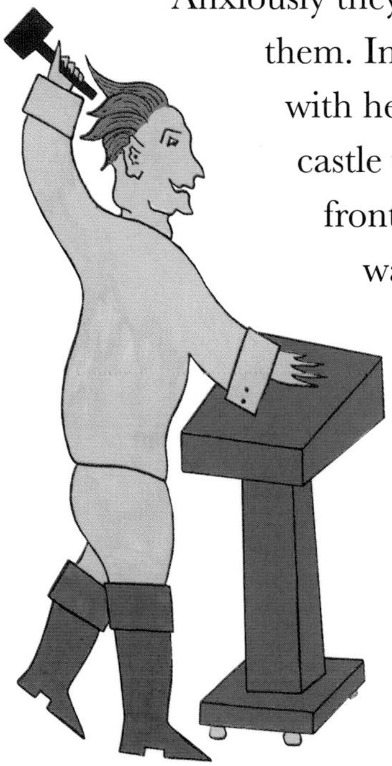

The bidding was fierce.

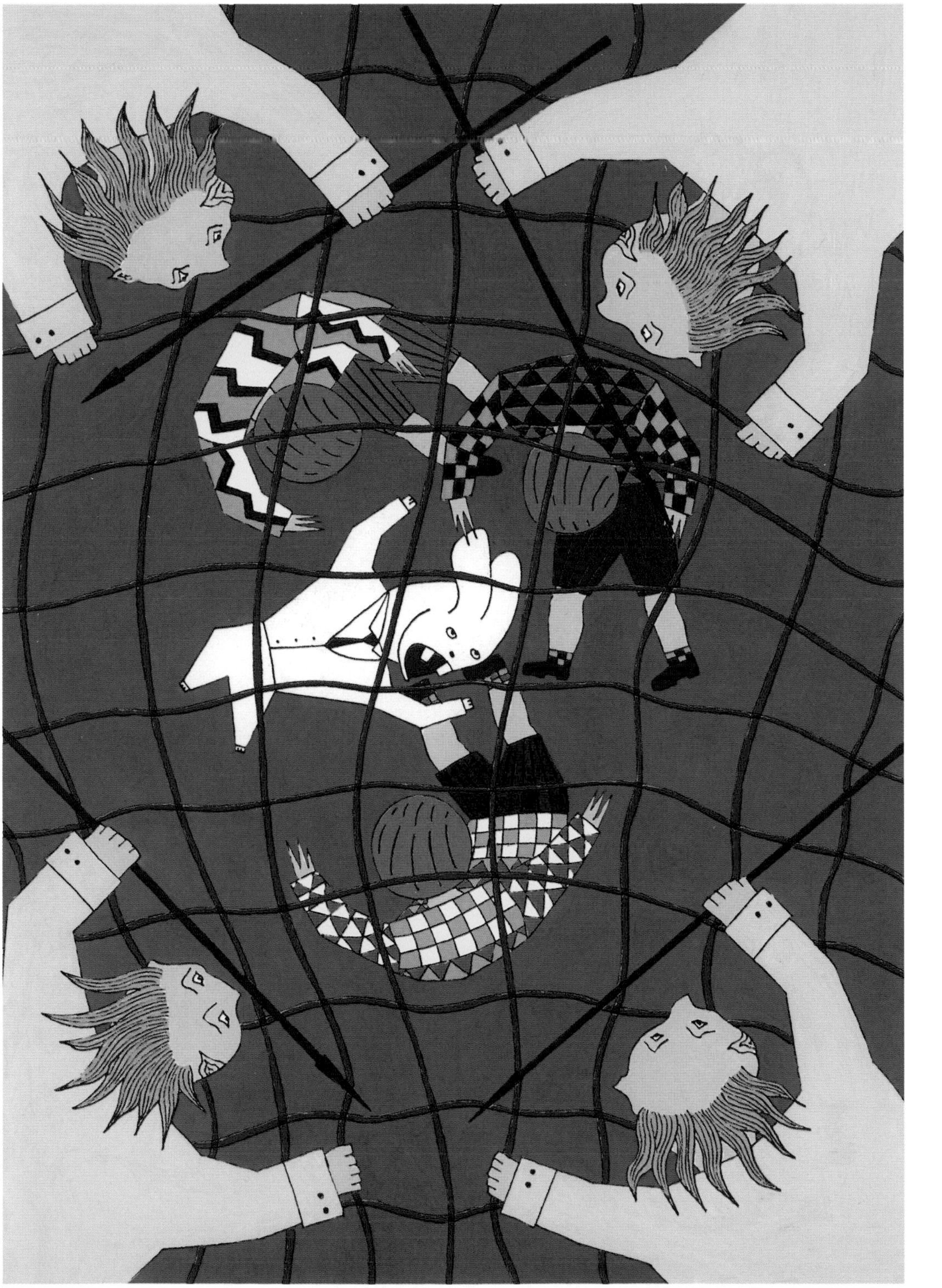

"£5. Will anyone give me £5?" Miss Poggenpop raised her stick.

"£10?" The fat man cracked his whip.

"£15?" Miss Poggenpop raised her stick.

"£20?" The fat man cracked his whip.

"£25?" Miss Poggenpop shook her head.

"Oh no," sighed the boys. "The fat man's going to get us."

Then a voice at the back squeaked, "£25!"

"£25. Will anyone give me £30?" The fat man shook his head. "Going, going, gone. Sold to the rabbit for £25."

Scrooey-Looey ran forward and handed over the money. The boys were free. They ran outside. "Thank you, Scrooey-Looey! But where did you get the money?"

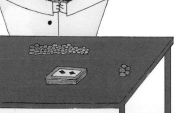

The rabbit yawned. He had been up all night in the lettuce bar. "Oh, just a few games of cards," he muttered softly.

The boys were shocked. "Scrooey-Looey! That's gambling! Mum and Dad would not approve!"

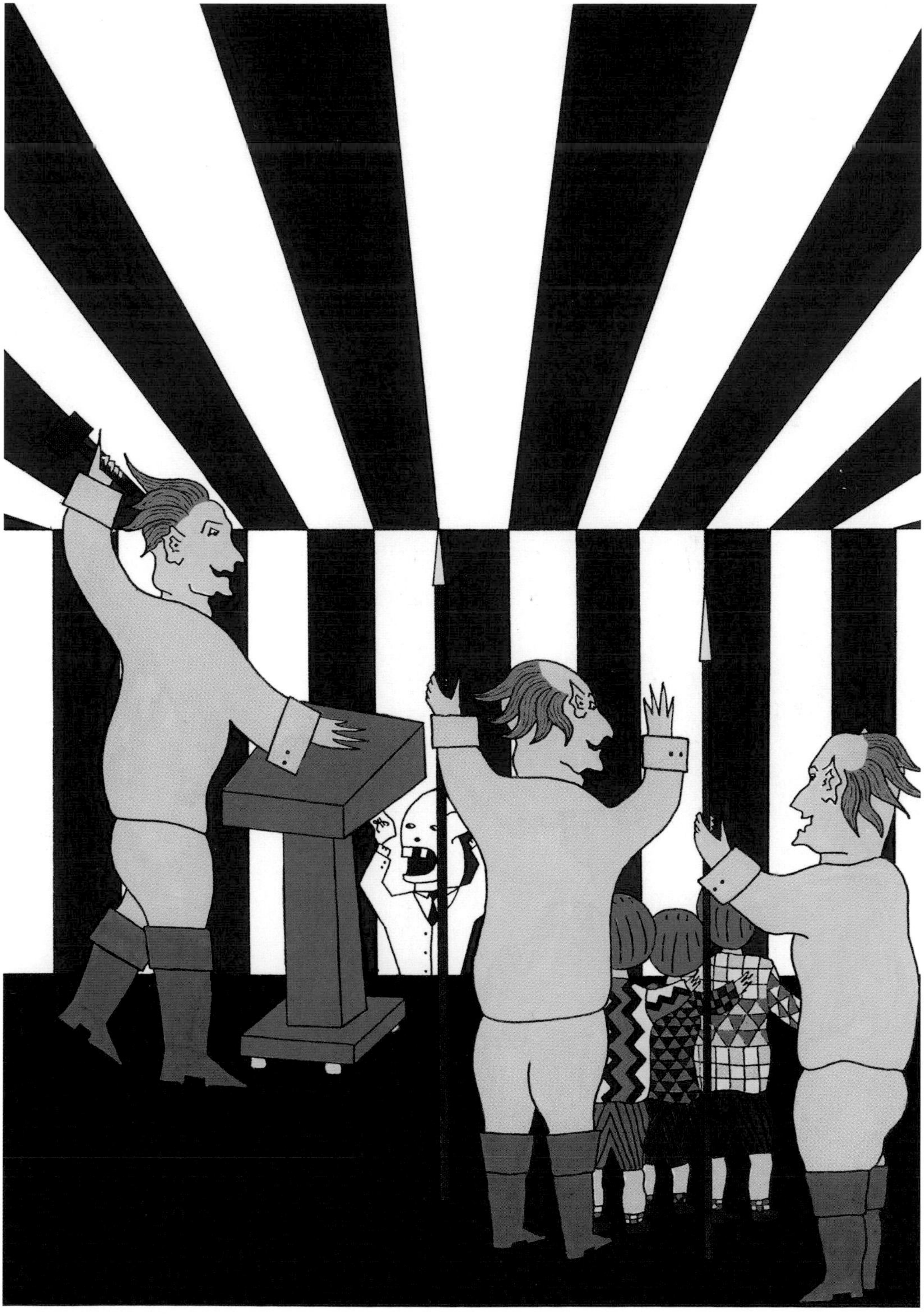

But then a loud voice boomed: "How nice to see you, boys. Do join me for supper." It was Griselda.

"Oh no!" the boys cried.

"Oh yes!" drooled Griselda. "This time I shall bind you up straight away." She pointed her magic staff at them, uttered a spell and heavy balls of iron, chains and rope flew through the air. "Got you! Got you! Got you!" cried Griselda.

But the little plants were still in their pockets and quickly reversed the magic. Balls and chains snapped shut around Griselda's wrists. She staggered under the weight. Rope wound up and down her body and round her ankles.

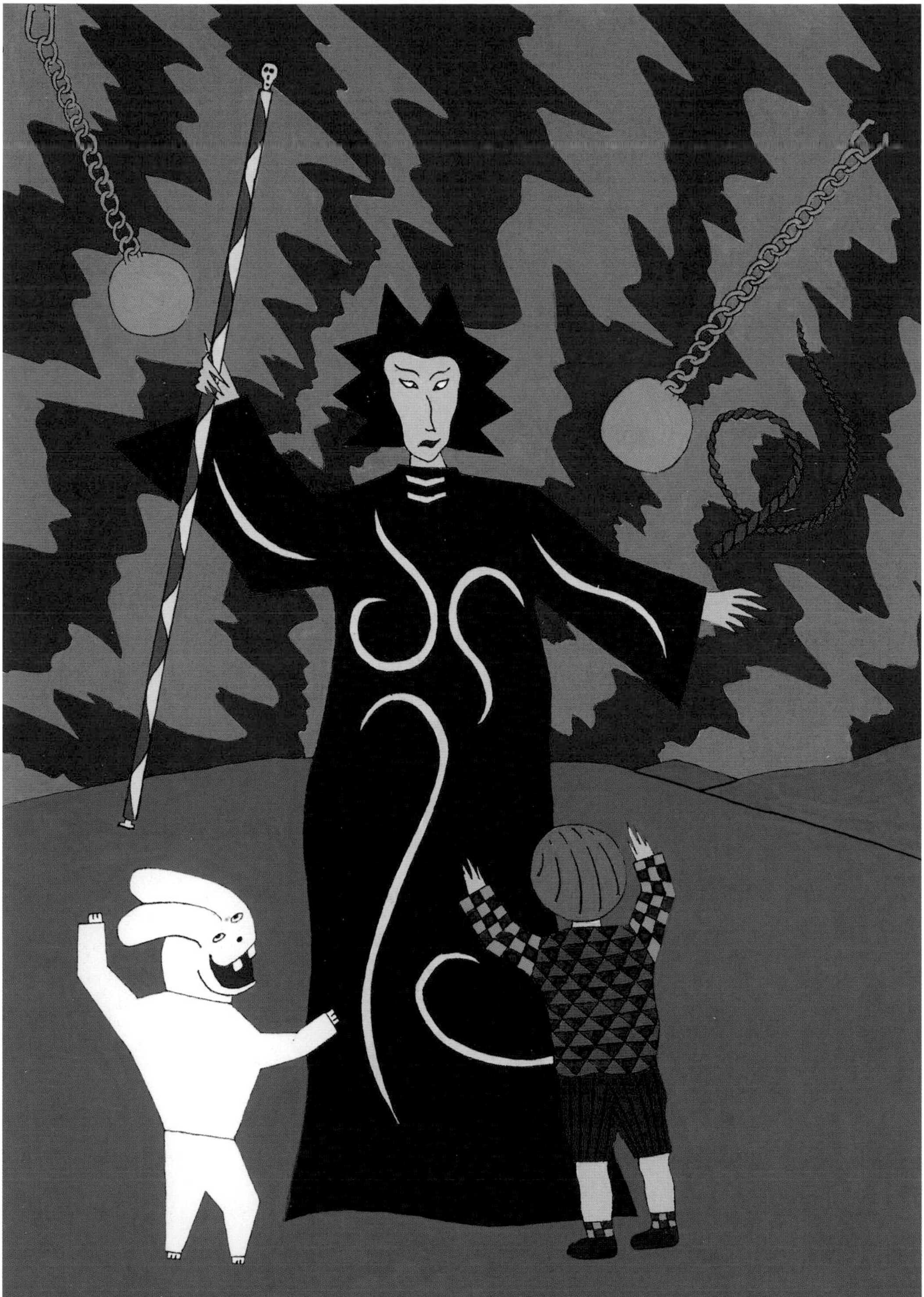

Scrooey-Looey picked up the end of the rope, and pulled it hard. Griselda swayed, tottered and fell with a splash into a puddle. She would have screamed, but a gag sprang across her mouth. "Mmmmm!" she mumbled, struggling uselessly.

At that moment Snuggle arrived. The cat was back from a hunting trip and had come to rescue the boys and rabbit.

"Snuggle!" they cried. "We are pleased to see you."

"We've had enough of this adventure."

"We've met all sorts of dreadful creatures."

"Can you take us home?"

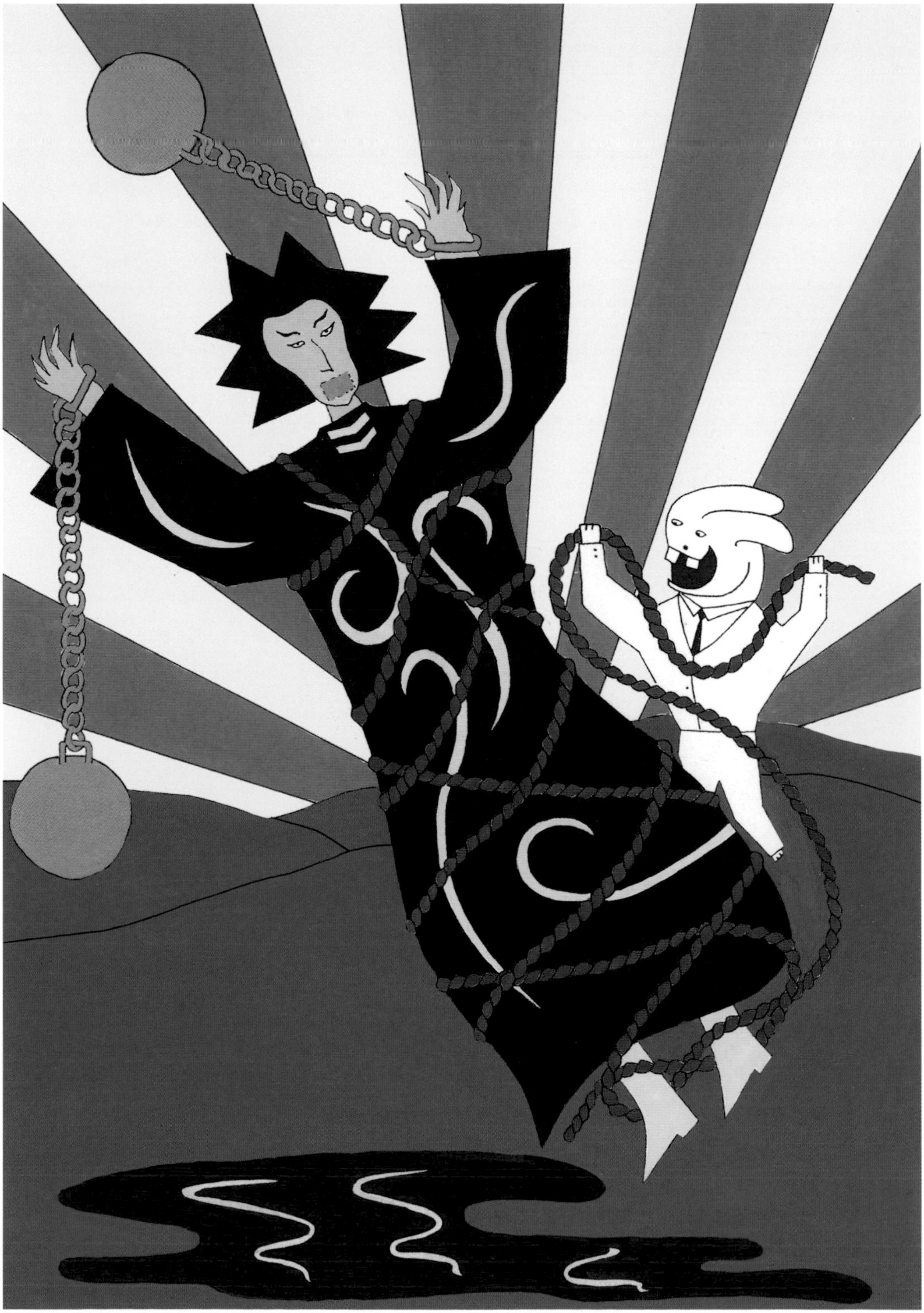

"But of course," replied the cat, giving a sudden roar and turning into a lion. He grew a pair of golden wings. "Get on my back."

They flew towards the Garden. The boys and rabbit laughed and sang. It was wonderful to be alive. Snuggle landed beside an open door in a high brick wall.

"Follow us," squeaked the Precious Plants, as they jumped out of their pockets and led the way into the Garden.

"Welcome! Welcome!" cried the Gardener. "You are just in time for supper. Then you must get home before you are missed."

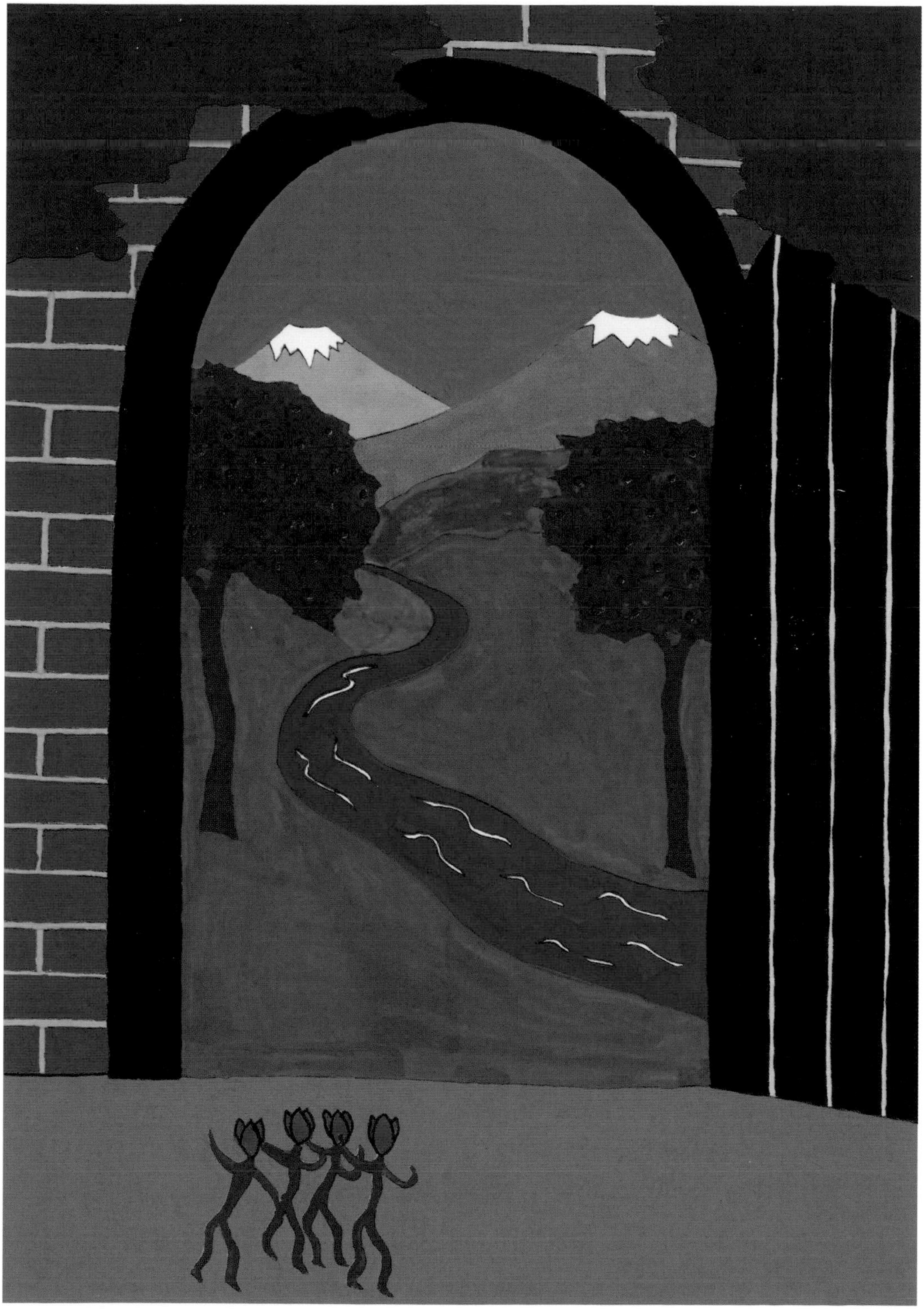

TALES OF RAMION

Blown away by Creatures of the Forest?
More magic and madness awaits you...

Available Now:

TALES OF RAMION
FRANKIE AND THE DANCING FURIES
Frank Hinks

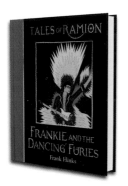

FRANKIE AND THE DANCING FURIES

A storm summoned by the witch Griselda (unwitting tool of the Princess of the Night) attacks The Old Vicarage and carries off the boys' father along with Griselda, the skull Boris (whom the Princess wants for her living art collection), the dwarves and the boys' mother as a child. The father's love of rock and roll distorts the spell and all travel to the land of the Dancing Furies where the spirit of the great rock god Jimi (Hendrix) takes possession of the father's body. When he causes flowers to grow in the hair of the Dancing Furies they reveal their true nature as Goddesses of Vengeance.

ISBN: 9781909938083

TALES OF RAMION
THE DREAM THIEF
Frank Hinks

THE DREAM THIEF

When the Dream Thief steals their mother's dream of being an artist the boys and their Dream Lord cat, Snuggle, set off to rescue her dream. The party, including their mother as a six-year-old child, passes through the Place of Nightmares (where butterflies with butterfly nets, game birds with shotguns and fish with fishing rods try to get them) and enter the Land of Dreams where with the help of Little Dream and the Hero Dreamhogs they seek the stronghold of the Dream Thief and brave the mighty Gnargs, warrior servants of the Princess of the Night.

ISBN: 9781909938021

TALES OF RAMION
THE LAND OF LOST HAIR
Frank Hinks

THE LAND OF LOST HAIR

The witch Griselda casts a spell to make the boys travel to her, but the slime of maggot is past its sell-by date and the boys and their parents only lose their hair. Snuggle (Dream Lord and superhero) takes the boys to the Land of Lost Hair, but Griselda follows, and sends giant combs, scissors and hair driers to get the boys. "Boy kebabs for tea!" cried Griselda jubilantly.

ISBN: 9781909938106

And these deluxe collections that include three or four Tales

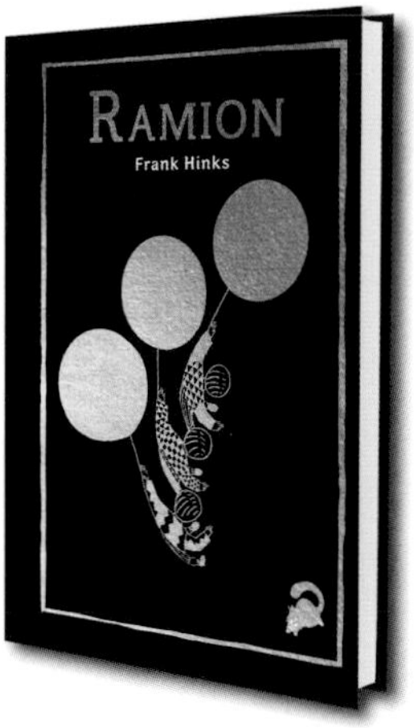
RAMION
Frank Hinks

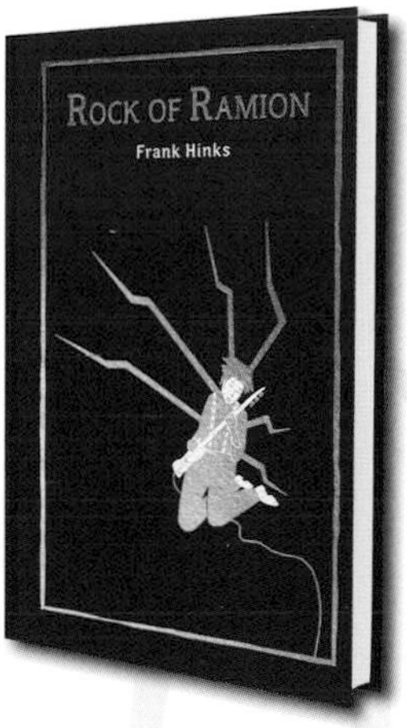
ROCK OF RAMION
Frank Hinks

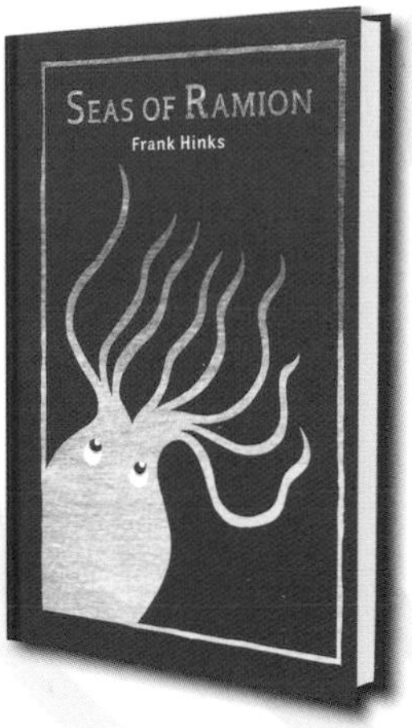
SEAS OF RAMION
Frank Hinks

RAMION

ISBN: 9781909938038

ROCK OF RAMION

ISBN: 9781909938045

SEAS OF RAMION

ISBN: 9781909938014

You can explore the magical world of Ramion by visiting the website

www.ramion-books.com

Share Ramion Moments on Facebook

TALES OF RAMION
FACT AND FANTASY

O nce upon a time not so long ago there lived in The Old Vicarage, Shoreham, Kent (a village south of London) three boys (Julius, Alexander and Benjamin) with their mother, father and Snuggle, the misnamed family cat who savaged dogs and had a weakness for the vicar's chickens. At birthdays there were magic shows with Scrooey-Looey, a glove puppet with great red mouth who was always rude.

The boys with Snuggle

J ulius was a demanding child. Each night he wanted a different story. But he would help his father. "Dad tonight I want a story about the witch Griselda" (who had purple hair like his artist mother) "and the rabbit Scrooey-Looey and it starts like this…" His father then had to take over the story not knowing where it was going (save that the witch was not allowed to eat the children). Out of such stories grew the Tales of Ramion which were enacted with the boys' mother as Griselda and the boys' friends as Griselda's guards, the Dim Daft Dwarves (a role which came naturally to children).

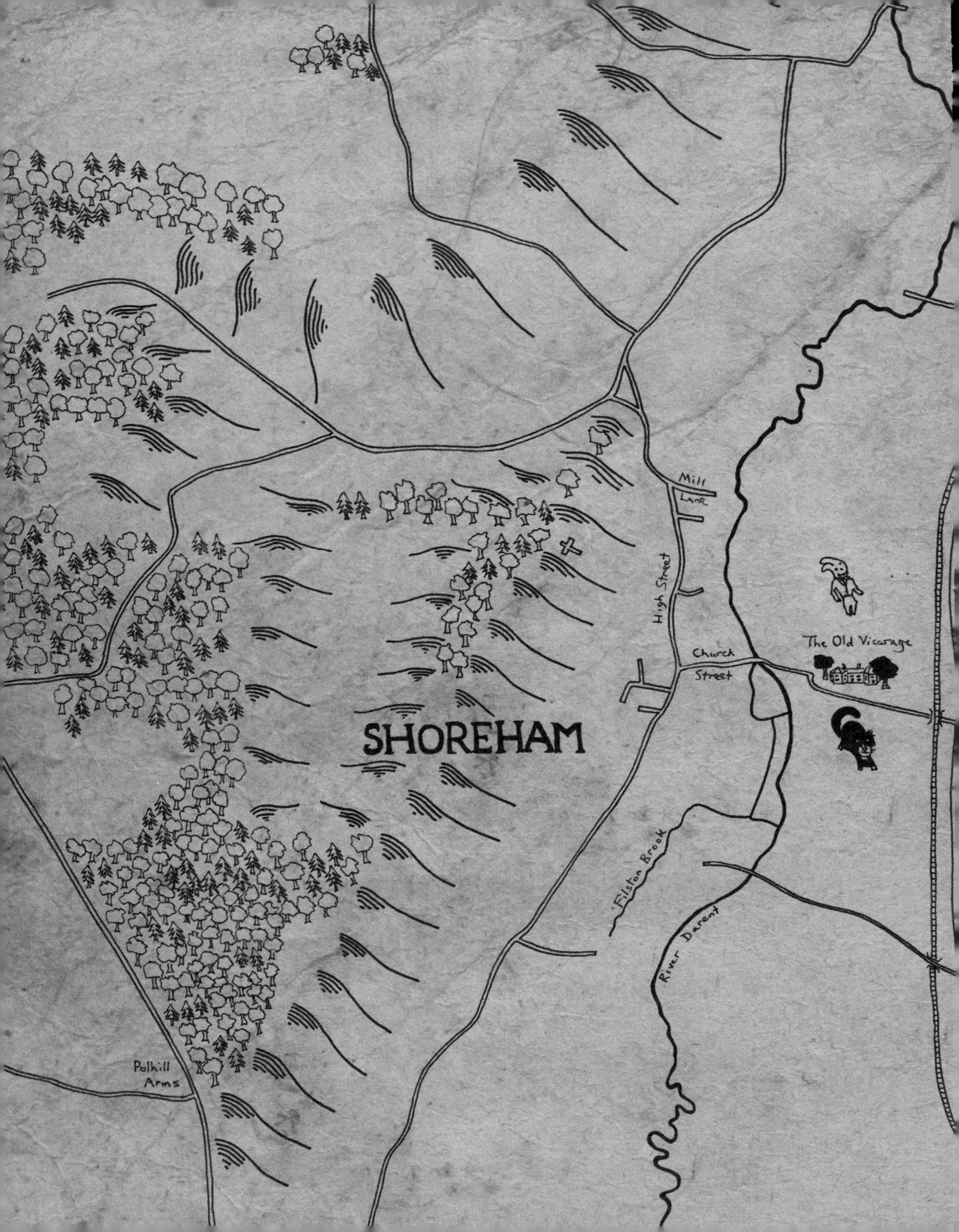

SHOREHAM
Mill Lane
High Street
Church Street
The Old Vicarage
Filston Brook
River Darent
Polhill Arms